ALSO BY GEORGIA

The Billionaire Banker Series

Owned
42 Days
Besotted
Seduce Me
Love's Sacrifice

Masquerade

Pretty Wicked
(Novella)

Disfigured Love

Crystal Jake
(The EDEN Series)

Click on the link below to receive news of my
latest releases, fabulous giveaways, and
exclusive content.
http://bit.ly/1oe9WdE

Cover Designer: http://www.ctcovercreations.com/

Editor: http://www.loriheaford.com/

Proofreader: http:// http://nicolarheadediting.com/

Hypnotized

Published by Georgia Le Carre

ISBN: 978-1-910575-16-1

You can discover more information about Georgia Le Carre and future releases here.

https://www.facebook.com/georgia.lecarre

https://twitter.com/georgiaLeCarre

http://www.goodreads.com/GeorgiaLeCarre

For Caryl Milton

Thank you so much for helping me even in
your time of great loss.

ACKNOWLEDGEMENTS

Thank you from the bottom of my heart to Nicola Rhead, Caryl Milton, Elizabeth Burns, Sue Bee, Cariad & Nichole from Sizzling Pages, Chelle Thompson, Sandra Hayes, Terry & Donna Briody-Buccella, Tina Medeiros, Sharon Johnson, Tracy Spurlock, Simona Misevska, Irida Sotiri, Lan LLP, C.J Fallowfield, Drew Hoffman, Nadia Debowska-Stephens, Maria Lazarou & Nancy of Romance Reads.

Hypnotized

Georgia Le Carre

The power of a glance has been so much abused in love stories, that it has come to be disbelieved in. Few people dare now to say that two beings have fallen in love because they have looked at each other. Yet it is in this way that love begins, and in this way only.

—Victor Hugo, *Les Misérables*

Contents

Prologue

The chick behind the counter smiled at me and licked her lips. Shit. That was an invitation if ever I saw one. *Sorry, honey, I'm married. Hey, I'm not just married, I'm in fucking love.* I had the perfect life. A beautiful wife, two little terrors, a successful career. In fact, I was poised to dominate my industry.

The results of my research would soon be made public and I was going to be a star! Life was good.

'Keep the change,' I told her.

Her smile broadened and yet there was disappointment in her eyes.

I grinned and shrugged. 'If I wasn't already hooked I'd ask you out. You're gorgeous.'

'I'm not jealous,' she said flirtatiously.

'My wife is,' I told her, and picked up the tray of drinks: cappuccino for me, latte for my wife, and two hot chocolates for my monsters. Suddenly I heard a man shout, 'Fuck me!' And though those two words had nothing to do with me, my body—no, not just my body, *every cell* that lived inside me—*knew*.

They concerned me.

I whirled around, jaw clenched, still clutching the paper tray of drinks as if it was my last link to normality. For precious seconds I was so stunned, I froze. I couldn't believe what I was seeing. Then an instinct older than life kicked in.

The tray dropped from my hand—one cappuccino, one latte, and two hot chocolates—my last link with normality falling away from me forever, and I began to race toward the burning car. My car. With my family trapped inside. I could see my beautiful babies screaming and banging on the car windows.

'Get out, get out of the fucking car!' I screamed as I ran.

I could see them pulling at the handles, their small spread palms hitting desperately on the glass. I could even see their little mouths screaming for me.

'Daddy, Daddy. Help!'

It was heartbreaking how frightened and white their little faces were. I couldn't see my wife. Where was she?

I was running so fast my legs felt as though they might buckle, but it was like being in slow motion. Time had slowed down. At that moment thoughts came into my head at sonic speed, but the disaster carried on in real time, slow time. Suddenly my wife lifted her head

and I saw her. She was looking out through the window directly at me. I was twenty feet away, but *I saw it.* I kept on running, but it was like being in a dream where your mother suddenly turns into a green elephant.

You don't go, *What the fuck?*

You just carry on as normal even though your mother has just turned into a green elephant. I just carried on running. I no longer looked at my children. My gaze was riveted by the sight of my wife. I was ten feet away when the car exploded.

Boom!

The force of it picked me up and threw me backwards. I flew into the air and landed hard on the tarmac. I didn't feel the pain of the impact. Coughing and choking at the smell, the taste and the heat in the thick, black, acrid smoke that poured from the wreckage I got onto my elbows and watched the fire consume my family, the thick, black.

Burning debris rained down. A small pink shoe landed within touching distance. It was charred and still smoking. I felt my body go into lockdown. It couldn't be. It couldn't. It could.

There was no grief then. Not even horror. It was just shock. And the inability to comprehend. The loss, the carnage, the tragedy, the green elephant. People came to help me up. I was shaking uncontrollably. They thought I was cold so they wrapped me in blankets. I wasn't. I was on fire. They sent me in an ambulance to the hospital. I never spoke. The whole time I was trying to figure out the green elephant. Why? How? It confused me.

It destroyed my life—past, present, and future.

Two years later
London

1

Marlow Kane

It was a bright cold day in April and the clocks
were striking thirteen.
—George Orwell, *Nineteen Eighty-Four*
(opening line)

'**L**ady Swanson is here for her appointment,' Beryl said into the intercom, her voice at once professional and terribly impressed.

'Send her in,' I said, and rose from my desk.

The door opened and a classically beautiful woman entered. Her skin was very pale and as flawless as porcelain. It contrasted greatly with her shoulder-length dark hair and intensely blue eyes. Her dress and long coat were in the same cream material; her shoes exactly matched the color of her skin. The overriding impression was of an impossibly wealthy and elegant woman. Women like her lived in movies and magazines. They did not walk into the consulting rooms of disgraced hypnotists.

'Lady Swanson,' I said.

'Dr. Kane,' she murmured, her accent polished.

'Please,' I said and gestured toward the chair.

She came forward and sat. Looking directly into my eyes she crossed her legs. They were long and encased in the sheerest of tights.

I smiled.

She smiled back.

'So, I believe you refused to tell Beryl your reason for coming to see me?'

'That is correct.'

'What can I do for you, Lady Swanson?'

'It's not for me. It's for my daughter. Well, she's my stepdaughter, but she is just like my own. I've raised her for the last twenty years. Since she was five years old.'

I nodded and began to raise the estimation of her age upwards. She must have been at least forty, but she didn't look a day over twenty-eight.

'She met with an accident about a year ago.' Lady Swanson paused for breath. 'And she nearly died. She had extensive internal injuries and was in hospital for many months. When she recovered she had lost her memory. She could remember certain things—like how to cook, or wear make-up—and, strangely, certain places and certain people, but she could not remember her past.' A look of sadness crossed her lovely face. 'She could not even remember her family.'

I nodded.

'I was hoping hypnotherapy could help her.' She leaned forward slightly, her lips parted. 'Do you think you could...hypnotize her?'

I watched her and thought of the men in her life. How easy it must have been for such a beautiful woman to get anything she wanted from a man.

'Lady Swanson, I'm not sure I am the right man for the job. Usually I treat people who want to lose weight, kick a bad habit, or who are afraid of spiders.'

'Yes, I understand that, but you *were* recovering memories, were you not? You had just discovered a new experimental method when your research was cut short by that awful tragedy.'

I froze at that.

Instantly her face lost some of its glowing enthusiasm. 'I hope you don't think I was snooping into your private affairs. I was only interested in your professional credentials...'

Even now the reference to my family was like a knife in my heart. I struggled not to show any emotion in my face. I smiled tightly. I was aware that search engines brought the personal stuff up with the professional stuff. After the accident the two had become inextricably entwined.

'Of course not. It is prudent to check out a practitioner before you go to see them.'

'I just want what's best for my daughter. And I think you are it.'

Some lingering, old pride in the method I had pioneered and been so confident in resurfaced. I clasped my hands lightly on the surface of my desk. 'I am a clinical psychiatrist, but you must understand that my method does not have any scientific underpinning. In fact, I am obliged to warn you that there is virtually no scientific evidence to demonstrate the authenticity of repressed memories returning. If anything, repeated studies have proven that using regressive hypnosis to recover memories can actually lead to the patient creating new material, a phenomenon called false memory. In some states in the US, any evidence that is gained using hypnosis renders that testimony null and void.'

'But do *you* think you could help her?' she insisted, undaunted.

For a second that heady memory of my first success flashed into my mind. How excited I had been. How amazing to return to something important. 'To be honest, I've never had a patient like your daughter.'

'It must be worth a try, then?' she pressed hopefully.

'You have to bear in mind that not everybody can be hypnotized.'

She didn't listen to that. Instead she broke into a smile. It was like the sun shining out from between a crack in a sky full of storm

clouds. Yes, she was obviously one of those women who could whistle a chap off a tree, but... I was immune to it. For two years I wandered around looking for even the smallest spark of the vibrant life that used to course through my veins. All I ever found were ashes. Even now this beautiful, beautiful woman elicited nothing from me.

'You will take her on?' Her voice trembled.

I knew she had manipulated me, but I was professionally intrigued by the case and impressed by her deep desire to cure her stepdaughter. I had prejudged her as shallow and cunning when she walked into my office. But she nurtured a deep and genuine care for another human being. A rare and precious thing.

I nodded.

'Oh, that's wonderful,' she gushed, but softly.

'I'll try. No promises.'

She smiled—grateful, triumphant. She had succeeded. 'I am certain you are the best person for the job. If anybody can do it, you can. In fact, I *know* you can help her.'

'Does your stepdaughter know you're here?'

She leaned back and looked out of the window. 'A butterfly wing is a miracle, made up of thousands of tiny, loosely attached pigmented scales that individually catch the light and together create a depth of color and iridescence unmatched elsewhere in nature.

Our identities are like the butterfly wing, made up of thousands and thousands of tiny, loosely attached memories. Without them we lose our color and iridescence. Olivia is like a child now. We make all the major decisions for her. The world is a frightening place for her.'

I nodded. 'All right, Beryl will give you some forms your daughter needs to fill out and she will also schedule an appointment for her.'

She smiled again. And I had a vision. Her in bed with her shriveled husband. It was not only she who had done a quick Google search. It was not every day that Lady Swanson, of the great Swanson dynasty, called my office for an appointment.

For a moment our eyes held and I saw something in hers. Interest. Desire. I let my gaze slide away.

'Thank you... Dr. Kane.'

'Goodbye, Lady Swanson.'

I walked to the door, opened it, and let her out. As she passed me her perfume wafted into my nostrils. Expensive, faint, but still potent. Up close, her carefully powdered skin was even more flawless. I closed the door and walked to my desk. I opened my drawer and taking out a bottle of Jack Daniel's poured myself a huge measure. I knocked it back, swallowed, and closed my eyes.

Fuck. Was it ever going to stop hurting?

Then I walked to the window and watched Lady Swanson get into her chauffeur-driven Rolls-Royce Phantom. She stared straight ahead. Distant, unreachable, from a different world. It was almost as if it was only a dream that she had come into my office and sat in my chair.

The intercom buzzed. 'Can I come in?' Beryl asked.

I sighed. 'Yes.'

The door opened even before I had taken my finger away from the button.

'Well?' she asked, wide-eyed. 'That was a very short first session. What did she want?'

'She wants me to treat her stepdaughter.'

Her eyes became huge. 'What? She wants you to treat her Lady Olivia?'

'How did you know that?'

'It was all over the papers. She met with an accident and lost her memory. You have your work cut out for you.'

'Why do you say that?'

'Lady Olivia is known in the tabloids as "Lady O". She has never ever given an interview and furiously guards her privacy. Unlike the other "It" girls, there are no pictures of her behaving badly. Ever.'

Beryl came deeper into the room and went to my computer. She typed in a few words and turned toward me, her face filled with gossipy excitement. 'Here. This is what she looks like.'

I walked toward the computer screen.

It was not a very good picture. A long lens photo. Grainy. And not even in color. But my cock twitched and woke up from its deep sleep.

2

I glanced restlessly at my watch: ten minutes
to spare before Lady Olivia's appointment. My
heart was pumping strongly and there was a
strange tension in my gut. I pulled the bottle
of JD from my desk drawer, unscrewed the
cap and took a long swig straight from its
mouth. The fiery liquid burned all the way
into my empty stomach. Heat sped along my
veins warming, easing, dulling. Artificially
relaxed I sprayed breath freshener into my
mouth.

Horrible stuff.

I stood up and walked over to the window.
It was late in the afternoon and the
pavements were already full of people
hurrying home. I had been there for less than
a minute when a Rolls-Royce Phantom pulled
up on the street. Then, even though I *really,
really* wanted to watch her slide out, I moved
away from the window. I straightened my tie,
shot my cuffs, sat in my chair, and twirled my
pen. My pulse was jumping.

What the hell is the matter with you?

*Behaving like a fucking hormone-crazed
teenager.*

The bell rang. I put the pen down and listened to the blood pumping in my ears while out front she was let in, asked to fill in the disclaimer form, and reminded to use the restroom before her session started. I glanced at my watch. Four minutes. I badly wanted to have another swig. I resisted and waited for Beryl's soft knock.

It came three minutes later.

'Come in,' I called.

The door opened and she stood in the doorway dressed in a tailored, gunmetal-gray dress, thick black tights and flat black pumps. How should I describe her? Petite. Blonde hair tightly pulled back into a ponytail. Heart-shaped face. Straight nose. Absolutely enormous, glossy, gray-green eyes. And a full, small mouth that she had painted a frank red. She was neither classically beautiful like her stepmother nor pretty in the girl-next-door sort of way.

But she was...intriguing. Very.

'Good afternoon,' I greeted, standing up.

'Hello, Dr. Kane,' she said and took a step into the room.

Her voice held that fey, non-aggressive, aristocratic tone of the British upper class, and her expression was a politely closed door, but her sexuality reached out like a long tentacle and *touched* me. I can tell you now, it wasn't pleasant. It was cold, sensual, compelling...and undeniable.

The Goat of Lust had me by the fucking balls!

I had never encountered anything like it before. I could liken the sensation only to the moment when a youth first discovers that he is attracted to other men. There is sadness and regret that he is not like everybody else, and dismay at the task of confronting his parents with the 'bad' news. Laced underneath the trepidation is intense curiosity, terrible excitement for the forbidden, and not an ounce of revulsion.

Right there and then I knew that under no circumstances could I treat Lady Olivia. I was too sexually aroused to remain detached or impartial. And I could only see the situation in my pants worsening with more proximity. The last thing in the world I needed was to court another scandal. Nothing good could come of it—for me, *or* her. I would give her *one* session and at the end of it when I had a better overview of her case, I would recommend a couple of regression experts whom I trusted.

I gestured my open palm toward the chair facing my desk. 'Have a seat,' I invited.

'Thank you,' she replied and began moving toward it.

Coming forward, Beryl raised her eyebrows and gave me an old-fashioned look as she passed me Lady Olivia's forms.

'I'll be out front if you need anything,' she offered archly.

'Thank you, Beryl,' I said dryly, but she just winked, and quietly closed the door.

I turned my attention back to Lady Olivia. She had just reached the chair and was slipping into it. For some seconds I stood simply staring at her, mesmerized, actually helpless in the pull of her sexuality. Totally at odds with her cool expression, her carefully measured greeting, her severe hairstyle, and dull, somber clothing, her movements were shockingly sensuous.

She actually reminded me of those insects that have no voices and communicate by vibrating their bodies. Her body was communicating with me. The touch-me-not image she had created for her new amnesiac self was not the truth. Behind the façade lived a supremely sexual creature. The clue was in the startlingly red, come-hither lipstick.

I tore my eyes away, dropped her forms on the table, lowered myself back into my chair, and faced her. She was watching me like a cat, dignified, detached, and unblinking. Up close and facing the light from the window, her eyes were like two slicks of liquid mercury, completely opaque. I didn't know it then, but I was as doomed as the Red Indians at the Fort Pitt siege who were tricked into accepting small pox infected blankets and handkerchiefs from their white enemies.

'Lady Olivia—'

'You must call me Olivia. Lady Olivia is too grand.' She wrinkled her nose charmingly. 'It makes me feel awfully pretentious.'

I grinned at her. 'Nervous, Olivia?'

She smiled back. Great smile. 'Extremely.'

'Don't be. It's painless.'

'Oh! Good.'

'Right then. Let's see what we have here.' I pulled her forms toward me and glanced at them quickly.

Age: Twenty-five.

Not on any prescription medication.

No to the illegal drugs question—or at least none that she wanted to disclose.

No to photosensitive epilepsy

No nervous disorders of any kind.

Non-smoker.

Alcohol consumption: Two to five units a week.

No allergies.

No phobias that she can think of.

In short—a model citizen.

'It all looks good,' I said looking up.

She was staring at me again with that intent cat-look of hers. 'That's marvelous. So you will be able to hypnotize me?'

'I'll give it a try. As I explained to your stepmother, not everybody is susceptible to hypnosis.'

'Oh.' In that one little blameless sound was a world of disappointment.

I leaned back, my chair tipping, and regarded her with a friendly expression. 'Tell me, Olivia, what are you expecting to come out of your session?'

Her hands fluttered. 'I suppose I want to be able to remember my past—or at least some of it.'

I nodded. 'Do you remember *nothing* at all of your past?'

'Almost nothing.'

I found my eyes roving her face distractedly. Her complexion was milky white and when she spoke she hardly moved her mouth at all.

'What do you remember?'

'My first and most vivid memory is of my grandmother. She was smoking a menthol-tipped cigarette in the Tapestry Room and she opened her silver cigarette box and popped one between my lips so I could pretend to smoke. I remembered the thrill of sucking on it, the cold minty air that came out of the filter, and her amused, indulgent expression as she looked down at me. I knew that she loved me dearly and I loved her just as well.'

'How old do you think you were then?'

She shrugged one shoulder, a lazy, sinuous movement. 'I don't know. Maybe seven.'

Her lips had not shut after she had spoken but remained parted and moist. A glimmer of perfect white teeth showed in the gap. And I suddenly and absolutely craved to see her naked and sucking my cock.

I coughed. 'How soon after your accident did this memory surface?'

'It happened at the hospital as I was coming out of the anesthetic. After that there were no more clear memories—just vague impressions of familiarity, feeling that I knew a place or a person, and unconnected—I must say, disconcerting—flashes of images.'

'Disconcerting?' I questioned.

'Yes. I'll get a flash of something and when I try to remember more I'll end up with a stabbing headache. My doctor says it's some sort of post-traumatic thing. At other times I get to a point then my mind will go completely blank, as if I have come up to a brick wall.'

I nodded and tried hard to concentrate. 'I see. What about dreams? Do you dream of the past?'

She frowned. 'Not really. But I do have a recurring dream where I am going down a dark hallway. I think it could the east wing of Marlborough Hall, our family home, but I'm not sure. I seem to be very young because my bare feet are very small and my toes are painted shell pink, but untidily, the way a child would paint them.'

Unconsciously she hugs herself.

'Then I reach a door and I am suddenly filled with a frightfully intense sense of impending doom. I want to turn around and walk away, but I cannot. My whole body is clenched and trembling with fear. I am so terrified I feel sick, but I turn the knob and open the door.'

She lifts a shaking hand and wipes her nape as if she is smoothing down the hairs standing up at the back of her neck.

'I find myself at the threshold of an unpainted, uncarpeted, desolate room. It is bare but for a rocking chair that is rocking all by itself. As if someone has just vacated it. I know from the silent fear that hangs in the air that something very bad happened in that room. Then I wake up in a cold sweat, frightened, uneasy, and with a strong sense that I am in terrible danger.'

I stared at her, surprised and unsettled. This was not at all going the way I thought it would. 'Do you see a psychiatrist?'

'Yes. I see Dr. Greenhalgh once a week.'

I nodded. 'Good. One last question. How did you feel when you first saw your family?'

She shifted uneasily in her chair. 'I don't know. I could hardly believe it when they said they were my family.'

'Why?'

'It just seemed extraordinary.'

'In what way?'

A strange expression flickered across her face. She clasped her hands in her lap. 'I'm afraid you'll think me awfully ungrateful.'

'Try me?'

21

She licked her lip and, looking me directly in the eye, said, 'Because I felt no love for them at all... No matter what they said or did for me.'

3

'**I** wouldn't call that ingratitude, Olivia,' I said mildly. 'Trauma can have totally unpredictable effects on the brain and psyche.'

She smiled uncertainly. 'That's what Dr. Greenhalgh says, too.

'Right. We'll start off with a word association exercise. I'll say a word and you tell me the first thing that comes into your mind.'

She frowned. 'A word association exercise? What has that to do with hypnosis?'

'We want you to remain as calm and relaxed as possible through your descent into hypnosis. That means avoiding any words that elicit a negative or ambivalent response from you. And since you can't tell me about any phobias or painful memory associations from the past, a word play exercise is the easiest way to excavate undesirable triggers. Bear in mind that some of the words I am going to throw at you have nothing to do with the process, but are in the mix to keep your mind free-wheeling.'

Her eyes shimmered. 'All right.'

'Once we have established your parameters I will take you next door and we'll start your hypnosis.'

She turned her head nervously toward the door I had indicated.

As I did with all my clients I immediately put her at ease. 'It's a soundproof room. All our sessions will be recorded to protect you from impropriety and me from any accusations of impropriety. Ready to start?' I asked, picking up my pen.

She took a deep breath. 'Yes, I think so.'

I turned a new page in my notebook. 'Sky,' I threw at her.

'Stormy,' she countered.

'Run.'

'Away,' she responded immediately.

I scribbled her answer. 'Painting.'

'Doorway,' she replied.

Odd answer. 'Doorway.' I said, looking up at her.

'Looking glass,' she tossed back.

Very interesting. 'Looking glass,' I called out.

'Danger,' she said without missing a beat.

I resisted the slight sensation of uneasiness. Her associations seemed disjointed and haphazard. I had no experience of such answers. She was not the normal patient I saw on a daily basis. Something was very wrong. And it was quite clear that I should go no further, but my professional curiosity was greater than any sense of prudence.

'Water,' I pitched.

'Clean,' she lobbed back.

That was her first positive association. I breathed a sigh of relief. 'Earth.'

'Sin,' she heaved back.

Wow! Earth and sin! Where did that come from? 'Dog,' I said.

'Growling.' Her voice was becoming progressively softer and more confused. As if her own instinctive answers were surprising to her.

'Staircase,' I ventured, my pen hovering over the pad.

'Falling,' she muttered.

I kept my face neutral, but I knew I'd have to be very careful whom I recommended her to. She needed help.

'Money,' I said softly.

'Death,' she whispered.

My hand stilled on the notebook. I looked up. Her answer had spooked her too. Her lower lip trembled and I felt a stab of pity for her. *You're not normal, Lady Olivia. And yet I am drawn to you the way I have never been to another.* I knew there was no point going any further, but I didn't want to leave it on such a negative note. I needed to break up the heavy atmosphere that had crept up around us like a dark cloud.

'Silk,' I said.

'Sheets,' she came back.

 25

'Good. All done,' I declared, and grinned encouragingly.

She leaned forward slightly and looked at me with veiled eyes. 'Is something wrong with me?'

'No,' I lied firmly. Her answers had clearly revealed a mental lake bottomless with mystery and a deeply disturbed inner world. I swung my chair to the side and stood up. 'Come on, I'll take you next door.'

I walked to the door, opened it, and waited for her to join me. As she reached me I registered two impressions. First: that I *towered* over her. She was much smaller than I had originally thought. Second: the inappropriateness of her perfume, a girlish, floral scent of almost sickly sweetness.

She went through the door and waited just inside for me, rapidly taking in the dim lighting, the faint scent from the lavender diffuser, the blinking lights of the electrical equipment, the zero gravity chair where she would sit and the armchair next to it that I would occupy. I closed the door and indicated the recliner.

'Have a seat.'

She moved toward it and gingerly settled herself into the black leather.

'Comfortable?' I asked.

'Very,' she replied with a tense smile.

'Let's see if we can get you even more comfortable,' I said and taking the remote hanging off it, pressed a button on it. The chair began to recline and she wriggled slightly. It stopped when it reached the ergonomically optimum position of locating her feet fractionally higher than her head. In that virtually weightless stance there was no stress or strain on her back, neck, shoulders, or arms. I activated the therapeutic massage function and her body started to move and shake gently.

'Oh, this is nice,' she commented, rotating her shoulders.

I handed the remote to her. 'Feel free to control the strength of your massage.'

She took it from me. Her fingers were very white and slender, the nails painted pale. The skin looked soft. She had obviously not done a day's work in her life. Our skin did not touch.

I moved over the console and switched on the audio recorder. Then I flicked a switch and a metronome based device began to glide down from the ceiling. I stopped it when it was a few feet away from her face. I spent a few minutes tinkering with all the dials and functions of the different machines. When everything was ready I went back to her chair and switched off the massage function. The room became very silent.

She sighed softly.

I activated the relaxing heat pads under her back and looked down on her with a professional, neutral expression. 'Ready?' I asked.

She nodded.

'Excellent. Let's begin.'

I sat on the armchair next to her and pressed the button that killed the lights. The room was now lit only by the flickering LEDs in the different electrical equipment. In the small, sterile space, her nearness suddenly seemed more potent, her perfume stronger. I could hear her breathing in the dark. It affected me with a strange cold anxiety. I took a deep breath. Just this one session, I told myself, and switched on the soundless metronome above her head. A narrow band of blue light came on and began to tick like a pendulum.

'The glowing light you see has an invisible flickering, but its flicker rate is so fast the human eye cannot perceive it as an intermittent flashing, only as a strip of perfectly steady light moving at a perfectly precise and rigid repetition. Its frequency has been set to exactly correspond to the alpha brainwaves present in the human brain when in a relaxed state. Staring at it will entrain your brain in the same way your television does.'

'The TV doesn't hypnotize us,' she said softly.

I glanced at her. Her face rose out of the darkness like a glowing blue mask. 'As it happens, it does. You fall into a semi-hypnotic state every time you watch TV, especially if you view it in a darkened room. The longer you stare at it, the more hypnotized you become.'

'Really? Why on earth did they set it at that frequency then?'

'Probably so you will believe everything you see and buy everything they sell. Shall we begin?'

'Yes.' Her hand twitched on her thigh.

'Please remain as still as possible,' I instructed. Stress on muscular relaxation assisted in disorientation since one of the ways humans kept orientated was to know where their hands and feet were. With immobility, those ties to reality were weakened and dissociation was more readily accepted.

I waited for a few seconds then began the induction in my 'hypnotic voice': monotonous, deep, and somnolent. 'Olivia, I want you to fix your entire attention on the moving light.'

She took a deep breath and attached her gaze on the steadily swinging band of light.

'Without taking your focus off the light, you will relax every muscle in your neck. Feel all the tension flow away... feel *all* those muscles completely relax ... as you go deeper and deeper into your trance.'

I repeated the same instructions as I moved down her body: shoulders, arms, wrists, fingers, chest, stomach, groin, hips, thighs, knees, calves, ankles, feet, and then back to the face: forehead, cheeks, nose, chin.

She was still staring with a blank, transfixed gaze at the metronome, but her body had slowly spread out and become heavier in the chair.

'You are now filled with a great calm. Your entire body is so limp and so pleasantly relaxed, even your eyelids are getting too heavy to stay open. It is now impossible for you to keep them open anymore and they are starting to close by themselves,' I went on.

Her eyelids began to flutter downwards.

I waited until only a crescent of gleaming white showed under her eyelids.

'You are now in a very, very pleasant state, completely disconnected from your body, and aware of nothing except your mind, which is floating in a dark so intense it has a feel, smell and taste of its own. Nothing can wake you up or stir you away from this safe, womb-like limbo. And nothing else matters but my voice as you gently drift deeper and deeper into your dreamlike rest. Completely let go and go deeper still.'

I stopped and allowed a few seconds to pass.

'Your right arm is now so light it will start to float up of its own accord.'

I watched her right arm slowly begin to rise. When it was as high as it could go I said, 'Your arm will start moving back down to your lap at the rate and speed with which your unconscious mind completely submits to my voice.'

Her hand reached her lap and I continued, 'When I ask you questions the answers will float effortlessly out of your mouth. Are you completely relaxed?'

Her mouth moved soundlessly first, then closed and opened again. 'Yes,' she whispered. Her voice was like the flutter of a butterfly's wings.

'Are you aware of your body?'

'No.'

I touched her hand. 'Is anything touching you?'

'No.'

In the glow of the blue light her face appeared pale, slack, and blank—the features flattened, the mouth gaping, the expression reminiscent of someone of very low intelligence. The rise and fall of her chest was slow and steady. Her hands lay limp and still on her thighs. It was the look and stance of a person under deep hypnosis.

Gently I lifted her eyelids. Her eyes had rolled up and showed white. I lay back in my chair, my muscles relaxed, and my breathing deep and even. It was not a well known fact, but during a session like this the hypnotist also falls into a parallel trance. A similar phenomenon to the way a group of women living together will start to bleed at the same time every month. I didn't consider it a bad thing as it meant the hypnotist could help entrain the subject into a deeper trance.

I started speaking again. 'This darkness that you are floating in is not powered by money, the sun, machines, rotating gears, oil, God, or anything you know. It is powered only by you.... It is eternal...unfixed. There are no clocks here because time is not operating chronologically. Time is fluid. Your memories are all alive. Nothing can be lost here. You can find anything you think you have lost. All the things you saw, heard, did, and felt are waiting here for you. Days, weeks, months, years they have been waiting. You are in charge. Nothing here can hurt you.'

I paused before I carried on. 'Now, I want you to go back in time and find a place you loved. A place where you have been happy in the past.'

A child-like smile crept into her face.

'Are you in your happy place now?'

'Yes,' she replied in a monotone.

'Where are you?'

'I am in the woods...in France.... My father owns this land.'

'Describe everything you see and do.'

'It is...late summer...perhaps even autumn. I'm not too sure, but it has not rained for many days.... It is hot and dry and the yellowing grass is full of grasshoppers and crickets. They are calling out to each other. Everything here is alive and growing.... There are dragonflies flying above my head.... They are so beautiful. Everything is so beautiful.... Even the deadly scorpions hiding under the stones. Anton says I should be careful of them, but I'm not afraid of them. They have never harmed me. I lie down on the rotting leaves and look up to the blue, blue sky. And I feel so happy.'

She giggled softly.

'Who is Anton?'

'He takes care of the grounds.'

'What's happening now?' I asked.

'The mistral wind is blowing through the orange leaves making them detach and rain down on me. I put my hand out and an oak leaf has fallen into it. There is a red ant on it. It is running everywhere in a panic, but I'm not going to hurt it. I put it down on the ground and watch it running into a hole in the soil... Anton told me yesterday that under our feet there are mushrooms waiting impatiently for the rains to come...so the earth will become damp...and they can sprout.'

Her expression was contented.

'I want you to leave that beautiful scene and to remember what happened to you two days before your car accident. Can you do that?'

She nodded.

'What do you see?'

She remained silent.

'Tell me what you see,' I urged.

Her face changed, hardened. A frown marred her forehead. 'I am at the hairdressers having my hair and nails done. There is a party later tonight.'

'But you are not happy?'

'No. There is a knot in my stomach.'

'Why is there a knot in your stomach, Olivia?'

'Because it is an Invisible Society party.'

I frowned. 'What is the Invisible Society?'

'It is a secret club...for billionaires.' Her voice was subdued and flat.

'And you are a member?'

She smiled slowly, an odd, knowing smile. 'No. You have to be a parasite or a scavenger to join.'

That was the first warning that I was going where I had never dreamed I'd go with Lady Olivia.

'If you are not a member why are you going to the party, Olivia?' My voice was calm.

'I've been paid to attend.'

I felt a sense of unease. Yet, it was my duty to walk her up to the dark mirror and see what was hiding there, forgotten by time. 'Where is the party being held, Olivia?'

'Underground. It is always held underground... In one of the iceberg houses.'

'What is an iceberg house?'

'It is a house that has many floors dug into the ground. They have secret rooms underneath the house. You could never tell by simply looking at the house from the street.'

'Move forward to the party.' I waited a few seconds and then I asked, 'Are you at the party?'

A slow nod.

'Tell me what is happening.'

'I am sitting in a pool of light in a dark, cavernous room. And I am naked but for a pair of shiny black stiletto boots. There are people in the shadows. They are arranged in a circle around me.'

Son of a gun! 'Who are the people in the shadows?'

'I cannot see their faces. I'm not allowed to.'

She breathed softly.

'What are you doing in the circle?'

'I'm waiting.' Her voice held the first hint of a scratch.

'For what?'

'For one of them to tug on my nipple clamps. When that happens I have to go to him quickly or there will...unnatural consequences.'

I stared at her face, astonished. What the hell? Was she faking it?

Once a woman had pretended to be under hypnosis. It was her way of acquainting me with her sexual fantasy, a scenario where I played a major role. But that was a simple case, so shallow in scope that I had actually dealt with it in the consulting room using light hypnosis.

It was almost impossible to resist the soundless metronome.

I studied her for a few more seconds. She was very still, breathing calmly, down in her diaphragm. No, there was no way she was faking it.

'Why are you at the party, Olivia?'

Silence hung in the air for a moment. Then: 'I'm not called Olivia here... I answer only to Velvet.'

I inhaled sharply. *I'm going where I shouldn't.* I shouldn't push or lead, but I could not help it. The words tumbled out of my mouth. 'What have you been paid to do, Velvet?'

She whispered something.

'I can't hear you. Say it again,' I urged gently.

She opened her mouth and I leaned forward.

Her voice was almost inaudible, but this time I heard it. 'I have been paid to debase myself,' she mumbled. 'Any one of these men can do whatever he pleases with me.'

4

Lady fucking Olivia was a high-class hooker!

It didn't make any sense. Why? Why would the heir of the vast Swanson fortune prostitute herself for money? I slumped back in my chair, shocked and oddly hurt by the revelation. And yet it made perfect sense. The word association game had exposed her glass-like fragility, and an inner world filled with secrets.

For a few seconds I debated what to do next. The answer was obvious. The hypnosis had been a success. It had retrieved her memories, albeit an unpalatable one with it. My duty was not to judge or solve any mystery. All I had to do was bring her out with her memories intact and send her on her way. I had paved the way and any hypnotist could take over now.

I looked down at her. Her blonde hair glowed a silvery blue in the light from the metronome. A thought flashed into my mind—I would never see her again—and I was suddenly overwhelmed by an irresistible crush of curiosity. Perhaps it was wrong to give in to that impulse, but I could not stop myself. It was as if I, too, was helpless and in a trance set by her mysterious alter-ego, Velvet.

What happened to her? What did she do next?

'What happens next, Velvet?'

'I crawl towards the man.' Her tone is robotic and flat. Devoid of excitement, pleasure, or joy. 'When I am in front of him I lie back on my elbows and open my legs. He inserts his finger into me and I—'

'Freeze,' I said, and she stopped mid-sentence.

I had ripped myself out of my own trance. I was chillingly wide-awake. This was wrong, wrong, wrong. I had badly overstepped the mark, but inside my trousers, my cock was rigid, the erection so powerful it throbbed and pulled painfully against the material. I shifted to ease the tension.

Never before in my professional life had I done something that was not beneficial to my client. This was the first time. I had been put into a position of trust and I had just abused it. My initial instinct had been spot on: under no circumstances should I treat her. She was in transition. She was trouble. Especially after this. I could never be impartial. I had never been.

I decided to take her through one more memory, a pleasant one, then I would bring her out and terminate our relationship. I wanted no more. I could not afford to get involved.

'Leave that scene now, Olivia,' I said quietly, but my voice throbbed with emotion. 'Let's go backwards, back to your childhood. Let's travel to when you were five years old. It's your birthday. What are you doing?'

Her face changed—that same creepy, child-like face came back. 'My birthday. There's a bouncy castle and a clown. There are a lot of kids around, but I don't know most of them. I start walking away from the garden. I am opening the kitchen door. Blanca is there. She beams at me.'

'Who is Blanca?' I asked.

'She is the housekeeper.'

'What happens next?'

'She holds out a wrapped box. "I've a present for you," she says. "What is it?" I ask. "I can't afford anything expensive, but I got you this," she says with a huge smile and gives me her gift. I tear it open. It's a doll with blonde hair. I feel nothing inside me, but I smile at her and open my arms for a hug. "Thank you, Blanca. I love it." She hugs me tightly and smiles happily. "Off you go then and enjoy your birthday," she says and I move through the kitchen holding the doll to my chest. I go up the servants' stairs and walk along the corridor. It's cold and dark.'

'Where are you going, Olivia?' I ask curiously

'I'm going up to my bedroom in the tower.'

'Your bedroom is in the tower?' I asked incredulously.

'Yes. I wanted it that way. I wanted to be a princess in a tower.'

Her face changed suddenly. 'Oh no,' she gasped. 'Someone has come into the corridor. It's going to happen again,' she moaned. Her eyelids fluttered and she whimpered anxiously. Her mouth twisted into a grimace of terror.

'You're safe, Olivia. You're *completely* safe. Nothing can hurt you. You're not there. You can watch it all from a safe distance. There is no danger now. Stay calm. Stay relaxed.'

She breathed out through her mouth.

'Are you alone?'

'No,' she breathed.

I stared at her. 'Who is there with you?'

She shivered. 'Can I go back?'

'Just tell me who is there with you?'

'I don't want to look,' she cried feebly.

'There is absolutely nothing to be afraid of. I want you to relax and go deeper into the darkness. Nothing there can hurt you. And when you are ready just take one little look.'

Her lower lips trembled and her legs began to paddle as if she was trying to swim out of her situation. I realized that she was in danger of being torn out of her hypnotic trance, which would be very dangerous. It would drop her into a deep depression, but I simply could not leave it be.

'Nothing can hurt you,' I insisted, my voice trembling. 'Tell me what you see.'

'I don't want to. I don't want to.' Then she went rigid. Her face was like a mask. 'The white owl is here,' she shrieked, her voice so thin and eerie I felt dread like cold water down my back.

'What is the white owl doing?'

Her eyelids twitched and she began gasping for breath. 'Watching me. Always watching me.' Her fingers trembled.

What the hell is going on? I knew memories that were too traumatic and frightening were hidden away and covered over with less frightening images. Even in hypnosis this was the brain's final attempt at protecting the individual from the trauma or the suppressed memory. The secret that must be protected at all costs. In order to avoid seeing the perpetrator the patient conjures up dream material or animals.

'It's all right. You don't have to go forward. You can go back to the darkness to where the owl cannot see you.'

I waited until she had stopped trembling.

'Can the owl see you now?'

She shook her head.

'Good. Describe the white owl to me.'

'It is big and white with staring eyes. It sees everything... Everything.' Her teeth showed her lips drawn back in an odd grimace. 'It *hates* me.'

'Why does it hate you?'

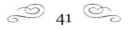

'Because I exist.'

I froze, stunned. It was not at all as I had thought. There was something terribly wrong here. All my assumptions were turning out to be a lie. There was a world of secrets going on behind the façade of wealth, glamor and respectability. She lived in a world of mystery.

It was far bigger, by far bigger than my fatal attraction to my patient. I glanced at my watch. Our time was almost up. I stood at a crossroad. Did I take her on or set her adrift? She was a prostitute. Of that there was no doubt, and yet she was calling out to me to help her. If I made a mistake with the Swanson heir another humungous disgrace awaited me. But I had survived that once and I could do it again.

My life was ruined anyway—this was my chance to do the right thing. There was a cloak of malevolence that enveloped not only her, but me, too. That sin had touched me and if I did not do something I would be responsible for its total and complete warp of her. It was not by accident that she had come to me. Once before I did not see what was in front of me, but this time I would not fail.

The mind buries memories that are too traumatic for it to cope with. It was a mechanism of sanity, preservation. Letting her remember what she had seen under hypnosis could bring harm on two fronts. First, she would have to deal with something she had no idea about. Her prostitution.

Second, and perhaps more important, I would almost immediately be accused of nurturing false memories. I needed time to work on her properly. I knew what I had to do.

'Walk away from the corridor, Olivia. Walk back to the party. Walk back to where there is cake and sweets and jelly and the bouncy castle.'

A smile came into her face. In the blue light she became a child again.

'At the count of five you will wake up relaxed and feeling wonderful, feeling so much better than you have done for a long time. And you will remember *nothing* of your journey back into the past. Remember, when I have counted to five you will wake with no memory of what happened during your hypnosis session.'

I paused to let it sink in and then I spoke again. 'One... You are returning into your body... Two... Sensations are coming back... Three... Feel all of you return... Four... You feel wide-awake, happy and energetic... Five.

She opened her enormous eyes and looked directly at me and I felt an electric current run through me. For interminable seconds we stared at each other. I could not tear my eyes away. My ears buzzed. And then I remembered myself. I pulled my gaze away.

'How do you feel about your first session?' I asked, standing up and touching the light switch.

Harsh yellow light flooded into the small room. The space was no longer intimate and bristling with sexual tension.

She blinked in the strong light and licked her lower lip. 'I think it didn't work. I think I dozed off,' she said slowly. When her eyes had become accustomed to the light she looked at me with a quizzical, puzzled expression.

I knew instantly what was troubling her. Women clients were always falling for me. It was natural for a patient to confuse their feelings of gratitude for feeling good with feelings of love. The thing that kept them at bay was my total detachment. But I had looked into her eyes just now and allowed her to see that she affected me. That something had passed between us. I had to put that distance back. If I was going to help her I had to draw the lines quickly, or I could totally mess her up.

'What is important after the first session is how you feel. How do you feel?' My voice was purely professional. A solicitous care for my client.

'I feel great. Better than I've done for a long time actually,' she admitted, a trace of confusion and sexual awakening in her eyes.

'Good.' I said decisively, and started to walk toward the door. 'When you feel able to, please join me in my office.'

I sat at my desk and pretended to make notes in her file. In fact, I was writing nonsense. I never made notes while the client was around. Especially when I had the recording of the entire session.

She came out and sat opposite me. 'Tell me the truth. That was a failure, wasn't it?' she asked.

I looked up at her. 'Not at all. It was exactly what I expected. I was laying the groundwork. We didn't do any regression yet. We will be doing that during your next appointment. The important thing is how you feel.'

'I feel great,' she said slowly.

'Then the session was a success,' I said and smiled politely. Awkwardness quickly stretched between us. 'This will be the end of our first session,' I said and standing up, started walking toward the door. It must have looked strange, but I just wanted it to be over.

She followed me out.

'Let me get your coat,' Beryl said, jumping up from behind her station. She came back holding up a long dark coat, its discreet silk and cashmere tag showing.

'Thank you,' Lady Olivia said, and slid her arms into it.

'Well, I'll say goodnight,' I said.

'Goodnight and thank you, Dr. Kane,' she replied softly.

I nodded and, turning away, went back to my office.

I closed the door and for a moment stood leaning against it. Damn it. What the hell was the matter with me? Why was I so affected by her? I walked over to my desk drawer and,

taking my bottle out, poured myself a large drink. I brought it to my lips. The liquid hit my roiling stomach like petrol taking fire.

Fuck! I needed that.

5

Beryl knocked on the door and opened it. Her eyes were shining brightly. Obviously she was hoping I'd throw her some little gossipy tit-bit.

'Forget it,' I told her before she could even come in.

'She is beautiful, though, isn't she?' she said, coming in and perching on one corner of my desk.

I sighed. 'Yes.'

'Did you have any success at all?' she tried again.

'Beryl,' I said warningly.

She clasped her hands to her chest. 'It's me. Beryl. I'm not about to run off and sell the story to one of the tabloids.'

'No,' I said firmly.

'You don't have to say anything. Just nod or shake your head.'

I looked at her blankly.

'All right. Be like that then,' she said sulkily and flounced out of the room. She popped her head around the door again wearing her apologetic face. 'Oops, it appears in all the excitement I forgot to mention that your cleaning lady called. She couldn't make it today. An emergency of some kind. She has to go up and see her sister in Brighton. She'll be around tomorrow.'

'Right. Thanks.'

'Well, I'm off then. See you tomorrow.'

'Yeah, see you tomorrow.'

I heard the front door shut and the place took on the waiting silence of abandoned houses. I poured myself three fingers of whiskey, and took a large swallow. Soon everything would become mellow. I leaned back in my chair and swiveled it around to face the window. People were hunched into their coats and hurrying home. Sitting here alone, I had watched this scene so many times. Until the streets emptied, and then I would pack up and go out for a solitary meal. Usually the Italian around the corner. They knew me there. *Il Americano*—the American—they called me.

I always had the same. Penne arrabiata to start and then Franco would bring out the day's special, whatever it was. Fish, rabbit, pig's trotters, sweetbreads.

After a few meals Franco had said, 'Always you eat alone. Big, beautiful man like you. Why?'

'Nobody wants me,' I joked.

He had jerked his head back with exaggerated violence as if recoiling from a striking snake. 'Nooooo,' he cried. It was the longest, most horrified no I'd ever heard. 'Big, beautiful man like you. Not *possibile*.' He pulled a chair out and sat beside me and with a conspiratorial nod said, 'I have beautiful girl for you.'

'Just the penne arrabiata tonight, I think.'

He moved away toward the kitchen with a wounded air. It was a few weeks before he forgave me and I became *il Americano* again. But I like Italians. Everything is so dramatic. They behave as if they are in an open air opera. Everything can be solved with a passionate declaration of love.

On the days I did not go to Franco's I would go to the gym and work out for two hours then end up somewhere more glamorous.

But one thing never changed. I always dined alone. I always went home alone.

Tonight my dick felt heavy and turgid. I was not in the mood for food. I phoned Jenny. That's not her real name by the way. Her birth name was unpronounceable.

'Marlow,' she answered immediately, her voice husky and full of promise. It never failed to strike me, every time I heard it at the end of a phone, how deceiving it was. In truth she was a simple, uncomplicated girl to whom life had been horribly cruel.

'Can I come around?' I asked.

'Of course,' she said. 'Can you come in...say, one hour?'

'See you in an hour.'

I placed the phone on the table and watched the pedestrians go by while I worked

my way down the whiskey bottle. This was me unwinding after an awful day at the office. The whole time I kept my mind obstinately blank. I never allowed myself to think of her.

When the telephone rang I was already half a bottle deep and starting to feel a little sloshed so I ignored it. The answer machine clicked on. A woman left a message. She wanted to make an appointment to see the resident hypnotist. 'That'll be me, darlin',' I slurred to the empty office. She left her number and her name.

Twenty minutes before my appointment with Jenny I slipped into my coat, and moving through the shadows of my office walked down the stairs and out into the corridor I shared with the other practitioners in the building. It was as silent as a morgue. Everyone—the dentist on the first floor, the jiu jitsu master masseur and the chiropractor, along with their staff—had gone home. I locked my office and walked the short distance to the thick, black main door. I stepped outside and a cold blast of wind hit me in the face. I smiled. Just what I needed.

I left my car in the underground car park and took the Tube to Paddington.

Jenny opened the door wearing a tight, V-necked, deep pink blouse and a pair of white shorts with frayed hems. 'Hello, stranger,' she drawled, leaning seductively by the doorframe.

I offered up a smile.

'Come in,' she invited, opening the door wider.

I walked in and took my shoes off in the hallway. It was an Asian thing. Everybody had to take their shoes off before they could enter her apartment.

'You haven't been to see me for a long time. Have you been away?'

'No. Just been busy, you know?'

'I've missed you,' she said.

Ah, Jenny. Poor you. I walked in my socks through her scrupulously clean home to the room where she conducted her business. It had a bed, a dresser, a well-used armchair and a basin and paper towel dispenser attached to the wall.

'Is it still the same price?' I asked.

'You don't have to pay,' she replied.

'Jenny,' I said tiredly.

'It's still the same,' she said quickly.

I took out my wallet, counted out fifty pounds, and put the notes on her dresser. Then I took off my coat, my jacket, my pants, my socks, and my boxers, and went to sit on the armchair. I laid my head against the backrest and closed my eyes. I felt a tight sensation in my body and my brain was wired. I needed to blow off steam.

'How have you been, Marlow?'

'Good,' I said briefly. 'And you?'

'I've been well.'

There was a pause. Her apartment was warm and the armchair was comfortable. I wanted to relax.

'Something about you is different today,' she observed.

My eyes fluttered open. 'Yeah?'

'Yes,' she said sadly and went out of the room. She came back in with a basin of water with a few drops of perfume. Flower petals were floating on the surface. She put it on the floor and I slipped my feet into the warm, slippery water. The sensation was heaven. After she had washed my feet she massaged them with warm oil. She did not try to make conversation again.

Then she pushed the basin away and her clever mouth closed around the head of my cock. Expertly she rubbed her lips up and down my shaft.

I didn't want to.

I really didn't want to think of Olivia, but she slipped into my head, forbidden and intensely alive and naked, but for a pair of shiny black stiletto boots. It was her wedged between my legs, her plump, red mouth stretched wide to receive the thickness of my cock.

She looked up at me with her mercury eyes, not innocent and troubled as she had been in my office, but full of raw sexual knowledge.

In my fantasy I called to her as surely as if I had tugged her nipple clamps. Her face slid up and down my shaft. I ejaculated so quickly Jenny made a small sound of surprise.

6

Olivia

*It is the time you have wasted for your rose that
makes your rose so important.*
—Antoine de Saint-Exupéry, *The Little Prince*

It was only when we had almost reached Dr.
Kane's offices that I saw the hole—as big as a
five pence piece—in my tights. Scowling I
stared at the tear running along my leg trying
to remember where I could have snagged it
when I was suddenly hurled into the middle
of a full-blown panic attack.

My throat constricted. As if a ball was stuck
in it. I started to choke, my breathing
becoming shallow and fast. My skin started to
tingle warningly: lack of oxygen. That
instantly upped the fright factor: I was going
to die in the back seat of this car. My heart
began to race, surely fast enough to burst.

Utter terror took over.

The urgency and intense fear that flooded
into my being had no basis in reality. Nothing

had happened, and yet it was so real it was causing my body to shut down right before my eyes. It would be hard to explain to someone who had never experienced such an attack what it felt like. Perhaps they would understand if they imagined being trapped in a corner of a burning room with no escape and watching the fire licking closer and closer.

The sensation was clear: RUN! NOW!

But of course I was totally frozen. Unable to move a single muscle! Soon I knew I would start sweating like a horse or I might even start hyperventilating and throw up. That would mean canceling my appointment and going home.

NO!

I didn't want that. More than anything in the world I wanted to go for my appointment. The back of the chauffeur's head was doing a dolly zoom in my head, but, ignoring it, I started to practice what Dr. Greenhalgh taught me to do. The first thing you had to do was fight off the cascade of irrational emotions that swamped you. The first line of defense was to slow down—thoughts, breathing, feelings.

Deliberately, I started a totally different internal dialog. *Slow breaths. This is not a trigger. So what if you have a hole in your tights?*

I took another deep breath.

No one is going to see it. It is nothing. It is absolutely nothing. Everything is going well.

I coughed hard and it felt as if that ball in my throat was expelled. Silently I repeated *All is well, all is well* like a mantra until the terror slunk away and my muscles slowly unlocked.

Breathing deeply I looked out of the window. The world outside me was unchanged. We were less than ten minutes away. I opened my purse and took my compact out and looked at my face. My pupils were still dilated and I looked a bit pale, but otherwise I was normal. *See? Everything is fine.* I closed the compact and slipped it back into my purse.

These attacks were coming more and more frequently and for less and less important things. The last time was yesterday in the shower as soon as the water hit my face. I couldn't breathe.

I looked down at the hole in my tights. It was still there. I ran my hand along the snagged material. I shook my head. *Silly, silly Olivia.* Then I twisted the material around my thigh so it would be at the side of my leg. Far less obvious. Perhaps I would keep my coat on. Not that anyone would notice anyway. Beryl was too star-struck. Anyone would think I had done something important or invented something hugely clever, and Dr. Kane was of course too professional and aloof. His eyes never strayed below my modest necklines.

The thought of the detached Dr. Kane was like a loving caress in my brain. Though I recognized that he was becoming something of an obsession with me, I could not stop thinking about him. He drew me like a moth to a flame. And a flame he was. Beautiful and bright but not to be touched.

Our first meeting was a shock to my system. Perhaps if I had not been so dreading the session, or if the reception area of his offices had not been quite so plain and ordinary, or if Beryl hadn't been so terribly impressed by my title, it wouldn't have been as startling when she opened a door and revealed him.

Backlit by the window he stood beside his desk, hands by his sides, the jacket of his navy suit open, a charcoal shirt showing underneath. No tie. His shoulders were broad and powerful and his legs planted shoulder-width apart. I had never seen a man look so rugged and powerfully masculine in a suit.

His hair, straight and so black it was almost blue, touched his collar and his eyebrows were thick and straight. Though it was impossible to make out the color of his eyes, they were harsh and urgent and, teamed with the tenseness of his stance, for a split second I had the impression of a gun-slinger, readying himself for a draw.

My skin had prickled at the threat, but he came forward, his manner cool and put together, and the impression became a fleeting trick of the light.

Wiped of all expression, his eyes were exact and penetrating. Like looking into a one-way glass. You couldn't see who was on the other side, but you knew someone was watching and assessing. As he came closer I saw his eyes were, in fact, whiskey with gold flecks glittering in them, and his nose, lips and jaw were so perfectly chiseled, they were as if cut from glass. He was an extraordinarily stunning specimen of the male species.

I had felt a thrill run through me. It was insane to be so affected by a man who had not even touched you, but God! I *wanted* him. I felt myself blush. Since coming out of hospital I could not remember ever feeling such an instantaneous and powerful attraction for anyone. My life was already a complicated mess, though. I most definitely did not need to fall headlong into a crush on my hypnotist.

He came forward as if to shake my hand, but he did not. Instead he waved me toward a seat. As I started walking toward it I became hyper-aware of my own body, the way it moved, instinctively, sensuous as a snake, totally unlike me.

But he was professional, precise and detached, and after a while my body stopped trembling with a strange craving for the feel of his skin, his mouth, his teeth. Just once when I had come out of the hypnosis he had looked at me, and desire had hummed between us. It was as if his body was talking to me. I felt it like a tingling between my legs.

Again it was he who coldly terminated the exchange. And after that there were no more such occurrences. He held his distance and made it plain that there was to be nothing between us except the sterile politeness of a professional relationship. We were to be two people who had nothing in common and didn't particularly like each other.

And yet I felt as if he was the only person in the world I could truly trust. He was my bridge to the past. The only one who could make the memories come alive again. When other people spoke of things that happened I felt no connection to it. Almost as if they were playing a trick on me. Remember when you and your brother put horse shit in a handbag and left it in the street for people to find?

No. I don't remember. Not at all.

I went to Dr. Kane and told him to make me remember the dung in the handbag incident. He put me under and the whole episode became alive. I remembered all the details in full color. The hay tickling my leg, the smell of the poo, the irrepressible giggles, the trip to the roadside, hiding in the bushes, shhh...shh...the sense of being so naughty, the way we had laughed, rolling on the ground, at their disgusted expressions. And then running like the devil. So fast, my ribs hurt and my breath came out in huge gasps. Finally standing in front of Ivana, and her eyes twinkling as she pretended to chastise us.

He gave me back other memories, too. Scenes with my dog, Freya. I saw her running in the sunshine, her shining, and I felt again the deep love I had for her. When I was brought out of my hypnotic state I was shocked that I could have forgotten such a great love.

Another time I relived the time I hid behind a sofa and heard my mother tell my father that she was dying. The matter-of-fact way she said it. And Daddy was so shocked he let out a grunt of pain. I remembered being so stunned I could not move.

And I remembered the first day Ivana came to be interviewed for the job of Mummy's nurse. I was five years old. She was dressed in very dowdy clothes, but her beauty shone through. I thought she was a movie star. We met in the hallway. She was on her way out. I stared up at her.

'Oh my, wow! What a pretty girl, you are,' she exclaimed.

I became cripplingly shy and dropped my gaze down to my shoes.

She went down on her haunches and told me she had a little boy a little younger than me. He was two years old. 'Some day I'll bring him to meet you,' she said. And then she brought out a box of gobstoppers from her handbag and offered them to me. Her eyes were kind.

I guess she must have pitied me even then. And when I lay in hospital all those months in a body suit because my ribs were so badly crushed, it was Ivana who visited me every day. Every day without fail she came. Always smiling, always encouraging.

Watson, our driver, stopped the car. We were outside Dr. Kane's practice.

'Thank you. I'll text you when I'm ready,' I said, and got out.

I stood on the pavement for a second and men and women alike turned to look at me as they passed me by. Wealth. It always drew the eye. I rang the bell and Beryl buzzed me in. I walked up the wooden stairs and entered Beryl's domain.

She smiled and got immediately to her feet. 'Good afternoon, Lady Olivia.'

I smiled. The first time we met I swear I thought she was going to drop into a curtsey. 'Good afternoon, Beryl.'

Her voice dropped to a whisper. 'There's still someone in there.' She made a face. 'She came late so her hour has run into yours. I hope you don't mind waiting a few minutes.'

I smiled. 'That's fine.'

She came around her desk. 'Let me take your coat.'

'I'll keep it for a bit.'

She stopped and hovered uncertainly. 'It is frosty out there today.'

I smiled politely.

She shifted her weight from one foot to the other. 'My sister made a fruitcake. Fancy a slice? It's very good.'

'Oh yes. Thank you.'

She grinned hugely. 'And a cup of tea to go with it?'

'That would be lovely, Beryl.'

She disappeared into the back and I stared at the framed painting on the wall that read:

Let not your past define you.
Let it refine you.

The first time I saw it I stared at it with a peculiar sense of weightlessness. I felt empty and sad. Like a ghost. The real me died some time ago. I had nothing to define or refine me. There was a curtain separating me from my memory. Sometimes the curtain looked so thin it was almost a veil. All I had to do was push the veil back a little. But then I became frightened of what lay behind the veil.

7

Marlow

I noticed that she had not left her coat at reception.

'Would you like me to take your coat?' I enquired politely.

'No,' she said with a smile. 'I'm fine.'

'I can turn the heat up if you are cold.'

'No, no,' she said quickly, a faint flush creeping up her neck and into her cheeks. 'I'm fine. Really.' She gave me a lingering look.

'All right. So how have you been?' I asked politely.

'Good. Very good.'

'Any new memories.'

'No, but I'd like to remember the day my mother died.'

I frowned, but I nodded. I didn't know what lay in store that day, but I could not protect her forever. Eventually, once I found out who the white owl was and why she was so terrified of it, I planned on letting her remember everything, the good and the bad.

We went into the room next door and she made herself comfortable on the zero gravity chair while I fiddled about with the necessary buttons and switches.

'Ready?' I asked her.

She nodded and I smelt her perfume.

I took a seat beside her and went through the induction procedure. It was now much shorter as I had already created the pathways for her hypnotized state. When she was in a deep trance I instructed her to go to her special place again. I waited for a few seconds.

'Are you there?'

'Yes.'

'Good,' I said planning to take her to that day next. And for some unknown reason my gaze skimmed her body and found a hole in her tights. I stared at it. Her skin was very pale in the blue light. I found myself blinking. Then I did what I had never done before. I put my finger on her exposed skin. My breath came ragged and trembling. What the hell?

I could *not* believe the potency and the force of my desire for her. I was powerless in its wake. The more I denied it, the mightier it became until this. Me touching her while she was lying on my chair totally helpless. And still my finger did not lift away. Instead it moved slightly. My finger was stroking her! Her skin was like the finest, smoothest silk. For heart-stopping seconds my finger remained as if unable, or more likely unwilling, to be parted from her skin. Then I snatched it away and closed my eyes. My hands came up to my head, my fingers raking through my hair. I stayed with my fingers clawed on my scalp while my brain went ape shit on me.

Fuck. Fuck. Fuck.

Everything I knew with total certainty about myself was in the garbage can. And then an ice-cold shudder ran through me. Very slowly I turned my head to the left. An unblinking red light was watching me, its regard unnervingly steady. I was recording this. All this was being documented. I felt so ashamed and confused. I felt like a pervert. I stood up and walked to the recording machine. I stood with my finger poised. All I had to do was to press erase. I should erase it. Here was enough evidence to brand me as a sexual molester. I would never work again if this came out. If I erased it, nothing of real importance would be lost. I had not yet begun her journey. I stood there another moment.

And then I put my finger on the erase button.

I pressed record and went to my chair. I remembered my priest in my church, his eyes rheumy and wandering around the congregation: 'The spirit is willing, but the flesh is weak.'

I sat down on the chair.

'I want you to go to the day your mother died.'

Her eyes moved under her lids.

'Are you there?'

'Yes.' Her voice was soft and distressed.

'What do you see?'

'I'm in a corridor. It is dimly lit. And it is cold. It is very cold here. I don't want to go forward.'

I stared at her, my own transgression forgotten.

'Why?'

'Something terrible is going to happen. I'm scared,' she whimpered. Her breathing had become irregular. Her lips were moving with anxious restlessness but no sounds emitted from them.

'Olivia, listen to me. There is nothing to be afraid of. Nothing can harm you. Pay attention only to my voice. Just take one more little step forward.'

Deep furrows appeared in her forehead and her body started shaking. 'Please don't make me go,' she begged.

To my horror, tears slipped out of her eyes and rolled down her temples. I knew instantly that if I went any further she was in danger of being ripped out of her hypnosis.

'It's OK, Olivia,' I soothed. My voice was calm and measured. 'You don't have to go forward. You can leave without feeling frightened or worried. You can leave feeling calm and in control.' I paused to let the suggestion sink in and for calmness to descend upon her. 'You are now going to take yourself away from that corridor and go back in time. Go back to one hour before. Can you do that?'

She nodded slowly.

'What are you doing?'

'I'm going to bed. Ivana is in the room with me. She is putting me to bed. "Sleep well, beautiful child," she says while stroking my cheek and hair. She smells nice. I like her. She takes good care of Mummy. "Nite, nite, Ivana," I say and she switches off the light and goes out of the room. I sleep.'

'Go back another hour. What are you doing now?'

'I am in my mother's room. I am tucked up in bed beside her and she is reading *The Very Hungry Caterpillar* to me. Mummy smells of medicine and she has no more hair so she has to wear the scarf that Daddy bought for her in Paris. The one with all the horses. She is so thin I can feel her bones poking into me. and there are blue shadows beneath her eyes. She is pretending to be happy. For me. By her bedside is a tray of food. It is half-eaten. My father comes into the room. He looks ill at ease. He stands by the doorway. Something about his manner makes my mother hold me tighter. Her protruding bones bite into my flesh.

'"How are you today, old fruit?" he asks awkwardly from the door. "Quite good," my mother replies crisply. "That's marvelous," Daddy says. There is relief in his voice, but he also looks uncomfortable, as if he doesn't want to be there. "Oh well. I suppose I'll pop in later to say goodnight." Mummy smiles sadly. "Of course."

'My father retreats and I turn toward my mother. "Mummy, are you dying soon?" My mother turns toward me, and smiles brightly. "Not tonight," she says and stubs her thin finger onto my nose. "But you can ask me again tomorrow."

'"Should I ask you every day?" She says, "That's a good idea." And then Ivana comes into the room. It is my bedtime. "Goodnight, Mummy."

'"See you in the morning, darling," she says kissing the top of my head. "I'll put her to bed," Ivana says. "Yes, do that," Mummy says, but her voice is flat and unemotional. At the door I turn back and my mother is staring at me. There is a worried look on her face. When our eyes meet she smiles brightly. "Sweet dreams," she says.'

I looked at my watch. Her time was almost up. I instructed her to forget the first memory, and then brought her out. She opened her beautiful eyes and trained them on me.

'Thank you for helping me recover that memory. It was very precious.' She touched her temples. 'Did I cry?'

'Yes,' I said standing up.

'I don't remember crying.' Her eyes were silver.

'Just stray emotions,' I said and moved before the moment could stretch, but damn, I liked her. I liked her way too much.

8

Beryl

To anyone who did not know Dr. Kane, he might appear aloof and uninterested in Lady O. It might even seem as if he was bored by her and couldn't wait for her to leave, but I knew better. In all the time I've known Dr. Kane, and I've known him for nearly eighteen months now, I had never once seen him look at a woman the way the way he looked at Lady O. He looked at her with the kind of longing that lusting after something forbidden brings. For her part, she blushed every time he even looked in her direction. But more than a month later and they were still no closer.

Enter Beryl the matchmaker.

I reached into the side-drawer of my desk and pulled out my make-up bag. Rummaging through the contents I removed my compact and opened it. I had not slept well last night and I looked pale, lackluster and in need of a dash of color. I dug around again in my bag, unscrewed a lipstick, and applied a fresh layer of berry kiss.

'That's better,' I told myself and chucked everything back into the bag. I zipped it up, shoved it back into the drawer and closed it with a firm push. Then I clasped my hands on the surface of my desk and glanced again at the clock. The session should be over any time now.

I looked over to the tray already loaded with the tea service and a plate of prettily arranged slices of lemon cake. Dr. Kane, I knew was partial to cake. My eyes strayed to the red light on my console that indicated the soundproof room was in use. As I watched it went off. Lady O's session was over and they were back in his office.

Right. No more dithering.

I pulled myself upright, squared my shoulders and walked over to Dr. Kane's door. I knocked on it decisively and waited. When I heard his voice, I turned the door handle and breezed in with a wide smile. Both of them, but especially Dr. Kane, looked up at me questioningly.

'My sister made a lemon cake yesterday. Would you like a slice with some tea?' I offered brightly.

Dr. Kane stared at me with disbelief. He knew exactly what I was up to.

Unable to hold his direct gaze I swiveled around to Lady O. 'You have to try a slice. I promise you, you'll never taste anything more delicious,' I babbled, the words tumbling over each other. To be honest I was unnerved by the look in my employer's face. Maybe this was a bad idea.

Lady O smiled, genuinely pleased. 'That would be lovely...if it's no trouble,' she paused and turned towards Dr. Kane, 'and if it's all right with Dr. Kane, of course.'

'Oh, Dr. Kane loves cake,' I said quickly. 'And it's no trouble. Everything's ready. I'll just go and get it.' Avoiding his eyes I turned on my heel and exited the office.

I switched on the kettle, poured the boiling water into the teapot and placing it on the waiting tray, carried it into Dr. Kane's office. Without asking them where they wanted the tray I laid it on the coffee table in front of the settee.

I turned around and addressed Lady O. 'I'm a bit late for a hair appointment so you won't mind pouring, will you Lady Olivia?'

'Of course not. Thank you, Beryl,' she replied in that polite, totally gorgeous accent of hers.

'I'll be off then,' I called gaily to no one, and quickly made my escape.

Olivia

You could have heard a pin drop in the silence that Beryl left behind. For a few uncomfortable seconds neither of us moved.

Then I stood. The suddenness of my action made his gaze skid involuntarily down my body and come to rest on the curve of my hips.

'How nice of Beryl,' I commented, and moved towards the couch.

'Yes, very nice,' he agreed, dryly. Poor Beryl. She was going to get an earful tomorrow.

I sat with my knees drawn close together in front of the tray and began to pour the tea. He did not immediately join me, but watched from behind his desk. My movements felt clumsy and jerky and I was very relieved when I did not spill anything. I placed the teapot back on the tray and looked up at him.

'Milk?'

'Yeah,' he said and standing up, strolled over to the couch. He had a really sexy walk. More of a prowl than walk. I dragged my eyes away from him and he lowered his hard male body next to me and leaned back with his legs spread wide. His trouser clad knee was inches away from my leg. Scent: warm man. How extraordinary, I wanted to curl into it. Every brain cell in my head lit up with the knowledge. His nearness in a social context made me feel jittery and out of sorts, like one of those cartoon animals that gets electrocuted and their eyes pop and all their fur stands on end.

'Sugar?' My voice was squeaky with nervousness.

'Two. Thank you.'

I dropped the cubes into his cup and passed it to him. I was mortified to hear the cup rattling on the saucer. My gaze collided with his, and Good Gracious, up this close, his eyes were the stuff poets write about, molten gold and piercingly intense. He took the offered tea. My gaze dropped to the discreet watch peeking out of his shirt cuff and his hand; big, the fingers elegant, and the nails cut square. Without taking a sip he put the cup and saucer back on the table.

From the corner of my eyes I could see him rubbing the side of his face reflectively. I leaned forward, my demeanor stiff and awkward, and picking it up the plate of cake and held it out to him.

He took a slice and bit into it.

I stared. And gulped. Wow! I could hear my pulse throbbing in my ear. All kinds of crazy thoughts were running through my head. I imagined his mouth on the tips of my breast, along the inside of my thighs, between my thighs where I had begun to throb. My reaction to this man was extraordinarily sexual and confusing. I wondered what was beneath all those clothes. I wanted to feel him with my tongue. I frowned. I couldn't understand where these bold and inappropriate thoughts were coming from. Were they coming from behind the veil? Was I a very sexual being?

'Are you all right?' He was staring at me. A single frown line furrowed his forehead.

'Yes, absolutely' I choked, horribly embarrassed. I turned away from him, hastily picked up a slice of cake, and took a bite out of it. It tasted of nothing in my mouth. It could have been sawdust I was chewing. I tried desperately to find something to talk about, but there was not a single thing in my head I could find to say. I swallowed the tasteless lump and reached for my cup. Taking a sip I dared a sideways glance at him.

'This cake is absolutely delicious,' I said.

'Absolutely,' he agreed quietly, popping the rest of his cake into his mouth.

I put the cup down and licked my lower lip. 'Do you like being a hypnotherapist?'

The frown was back. 'It is what I do at the moment,' he replied.

I was both curious and consumed by an intense curiosity about him. 'So you don't like it?'

'Let's just say it's a temporary fix.' His voice discouraged any further questioning.

I smoothed down the wrinkles in my skirt as if doing so could smoothen out my thoughts. When I looked up he was staring at my hands.

'What?' I asked.

'You have such delicate little hands. I bet all the boys fall over themselves to protect you,' he said softly.

'I don't remember any boys wanting to protect me,' I said, nervously rolling the buttery orbs on the two string pearl necklace around my throat between my fingers.

His eyes flashed. He moved forward suddenly and rested his forearms on his thighs. 'To be honest, I'm not really a tea person. If you don't mind I'll have a whiskey.'

'Not at all.'

He stood and went to his desk. I watched him pour himself a generous measure of whiskey, and while still behind the desk, take a long mouthful. He made his way back to the couch more warily and sat down closer to the arm of the couch, significantly further away from me.

I leaned back and turned my head in his direction. He was looking into his drink and there was only one word to describe his eyelashes—lush. Seen from that angle they undid all his efforts to be taciturn, armored and completely impenetrable. He was like a peeled snail, achingly vulnerable. It made me want to stroke the tanned skin stretched across his cheekbone. He looked up suddenly. The silence stretched, holding within its body more than words we could have said. The air seemed thick with something. Our bodies were talking to each other.

But we both knew. Our politeness and evasion of the unspoken was chilling because it appeared to be set in concrete. As if it was the proper order of things that we were two people who could never be anything but strangers, unable even to carry a normal conversation.

A sense of urgency overtook me. Soon even this moment would be gone, squandered away. It was already nearly over. I turned toward him, determined not to let in end this way.

'My sister told me a joke today,' I said.

His eyebrows rose.

'A filthy one.'

One side of his lips curved upward, sensual and unbelievably inviting.

'Want to hear it?' I asked with a cheeky look.

That beautiful smile widened. 'Of course.'

'OK. A German Shepherd and a terrier meet at the vet. The terrier looks so sad so that the German Shepherd asks it why it is there. The terrier says, "I'm here because last night after my mistress came out of the bath she bent down to towel dry her feet, and her bum cheeks looked so smooth and inviting I jumped up and bit one of them." The German Shepherd shakes his head in surprise; "By golly, almost the same thing happened to me. My mistress bent down after her bath, but in my case I jumped up on her back and gave her one." The terrier is shocked. "Oh my God," he says. "So you're here to be put down too."

Exactly as my sister had done I curled my fingers in towards my palms so they looked like paws, and looked at them while I delivered the punch line. 'The German Shepherd says, "Oh no, I'm just here to have my nails done."'

I turned to look at him and he was laughing. Really laughing. Body relaxed. Mouth open. Beautiful straight teeth on show. Warmth and joy flowed out of him. I laughed too. And suddenly I knew it could be so different with us. So different.

Our eyes touched and locked. He stopped laughing. For a few seconds we stared at each other, a current of super-charged energy sizzling through us. His eyes widened slightly. Then he stood, his movement abrupt and final.

'It's getting late. I'll show you out.'

9

Olivia

Two days later a woman called.

'Vivi,' she gushed down the line. 'It's me, Cookie.'

It turned out Cookie was Lady Cressida Drummond-Willoughby. We went to school together and she was 'dying' to meet up. Dr. Greenhalgh had told me to mix with as many people from my past as possible. 'You never know who might trigger a memory,' she said.

So I told Cookie, of course, I'd like to meet up, but I warned her that in all probability I wouldn't be able to recognize her and she'd have to come up to me.

We agreed to meet at eight in the Beaufort Bar.

I arrived ten minutes early and walked into the newly refurbished Savoy Hotel and headed for the Beaufort Bar. It was unashamedly glamorous with art deco inspired chandeliers, antique mirrors, luxurious mohair upholstering and gold leaf backed tortoiseshell Lucite walls. The place was made for seduction. As I stood at the entrance uncertainly, I had a sudden déjà vu: I've been here before.

Cookie had said she would book one of the booths, but I decided to wait for her at the bar. I turned toward the spectacularly lit bar and did a double take. For a second I could not believe my eyes: Dr. Kane was sitting alone at the bar nursing a large measure of amber liquid.

He didn't see me and my first thought was that I should leave him alone. His posture was deliberately excluding and insular. And then I reasoned that it would be rude not to at least say hello. What if he turned his head and saw me? He'd think I had snubbed him. Besides, I was itching to talk to him in this place made for seduction. In fact, my legs were walking up to him even before the decision was consciously made.

'Hello,' I said. 'Fancy meeting you here.'

He raised his head slowly, his body stiffening. 'Fancy,' he said, and there was not a trace of welcome in his voice.

'You must let me buy you a thank you drink,' I plowed on, determined not to be put off my mission. With a smile I slipped onto the seat next to his and put my bag on the bar top.

'That's not necessary. I'm just doing what I've been paid to do.'

I looked at him. 'You don't like me at all, do you?'

His eyes were hooded, his voice flat. 'Don't take it personally, but I don't get involved with clients.'

My pride came to the rescue. 'I won't. I am here to meet a friend. She is late and I'm just passing time. You are hardly *getting involved* by accepting a drink, are you, Dr. Kane?'

He lifted his drink to his mouth. 'In that case, thanks.'

I smiled tightly through my hurt.

The bartender was making his way toward me. I ordered a repeat order for Dr. Kane and a dry Martini for myself. He politely informed me that house gin was Bombay Sapphire, but a smoother Martini would be got using Tanqueray. I agreed readily and he nodded approvingly.

I turned to Dr. Kane. 'Do you come to the Savoy often?' I asked.

'No.'

'Right,' I said. This was like pulling teeth. There was an awkward silence. 'Are you just having a drink or dining, too?'

'Dining,' he said.

The bartender arrived with our drinks and I made eye contact with him. 'Could you please show me to Lady Cressida's booth?'

His eyes changed. I was no longer the woman who had pushed herself on to the American drinking at the bar. 'I'll be happy to show you, m'lady.'

'Enjoy your drink,' I threw casually to Dr. Kane, and swinging my knees to the side was about to slide off the seat, when his hand came out to encircle my wrist.

The sensation of his fingers on my wrist was like a jolt of electricity. My lips parted with surprise. The action was so unexpected, my eyes flew to his hand and then to his face, wide and surprised.

'I'm sorry I was rude,' he apologized, withdrawing his hand.

I could feel the heat coming from him and my skin burned where he had touched me. I refrained from rubbing it.

He smiled. 'I come here for the Omelette Arnold Bennett at The Grill.'

I stared up at him not knowing whether to stay or go.

'And I like the steak and ale pudding with oysters,' he added.

I made up my mind. I swung my knees back to the original place and looked at the barman. 'Perhaps I'll just wait here until Lady Cressida arrives.'

He nodded politely. 'Very good, m'lady.'

I picked up the tall, classic Martini glass with its elegantly cut, long piece of lemon peel, and held it up. 'To your good health.'

'And yours.' He lifted his glass to his lips. Good God! He was almost *edible* with that sexy American vibe oozing out of his pores.

I took a sip of my drink. It was perfectly chilled with just a hint of gin behind the aroma of lemon. 'Absolutely lovely,' I murmured, and looked sideways at him. To my surprise he was watching me. I felt my cheeks coloring.

'I've never seen you with your hair down,' he remarked.

I touched my hair self-consciously. 'I'm afraid that's about the only thing I inherited from my mother. Hair that's too fine to do much with.'

His eyes caressed my hair. 'No,' he disagreed softly. 'I think it's beautiful. Under these lights it looks like spun gold.'

Flustered, unused to compliments, I set my glass down carefully. 'You are very charming when you try.'

He put down his empty glass and sighed. 'And you're having a bad influence on me.'

I frowned. 'In what way?'

'You make me behave in a way that is not entirely proper.'

'I disagree. I think you have been quite the perfect gentleman.'

He threw his head back and laughed, but it was a harsh sound. 'You don't know me very well, it would seem,' he muttered.

'Why? What have you done that is improper?'

'Don't go there, Olivia.'

I licked my lips nervously. I knew then that our relationship was always going to be fraught. We would always rub each other the wrong way. 'Do you live nearby?'

His head dipped a little, a gesture that was almost mournful, and I realized that he must have had quite a lot to drink. 'In Rupert Street.'

'I know that street. I think I must have known someone who lives there. Which end of the street are you on?'

'Are you asking my address?' he asked.

I felt myself flush and stiffen. 'No, I was just making conversation.'

'Number 34,' he said wearily, and swallowed the rest of his drink. I had the impression that he was going to walk away and leave me there.

'Dr. Kane, why are you so angry with me?'

His head jerked toward me, his eyes wild, his mouth twisted. I stared speechless at the expression in his face. It was almost a snarl, but I couldn't quite tell what it expressed. I suppose it was similar to touching something and for a fraction of a second being unable to tell whether it was very hot or very cold. I could not tell if he was furiously annoyed or something else. And then the fraction of a second passed and I saw it for what it was. It was a raging desire. So strong he could barely hold it in check.

I opened my mouth to speak and nothing came out.

'Oh, hello,' a plummy voice trilled close by.

I couldn't tear my eyes away from his, but he broke the connection and turned toward the voice.

Cookie. Talk about bad timing. Reluctantly, I turned to face her. A terribly smart woman was standing next to us. My gaze ran quickly over her: attractive face, a shining pageboy bob and trim, horse-rider body clad in a divinely tailored gray and red dress. She was beaming at me, but oh dear, there was not one thing about her I recognized. I sighed inwardly. Oh well, it was going to be a long night.

'Don't you look super!' she exclaimed, before turning her eyes back to Dr. Kane, the merest hint of a smile, like a delicious scandal, playing on her lips. 'I'll say, you're a quick worker. Who on earth is this? You'd better introduce us.'

I introduced them unenthusiastically.

'How lovely to meet you,' Dr. Kane said politely, offering his hand. His eyes were once again returned to one-way mirrors.

'How do you do?' Cookie replied with a breathless laugh. I watched her hand disappear into his large one and remain there, only releasing seconds before they slipped into impropriety. Oh my God, she was flirting with him... *Little two-faced bitch.*

The ferocity of the thought shocked and horrified me. It was like an ice pick straight into my heart. I dropped my eyes so they would not see how madly jealous I was.

Of course, she invited him to join us, but to my immense relief, he declined her offer. I could not possibly have sat and watched her flirt with him for another minute. Bidding us goodnight, he went to his dinner.

As we walked to our booth, Cookie turned to me with bright eyes. 'Sorry to barge in on your tender scene.'

'There was nothing to barge in on,' I denied.

She gave me a guarded look. 'That's all right then. Still, he is rather dishy for an NOCD.'

'NOCD?' I asked, puzzled.

She gave me a funny look as if she had just realized that it was going to be a difficult night. 'Not Our Class, Darling,' she explained with a patronizing smile.

10

Olivia

I woke up early the next morning and lay on my bed. My mobile phone was blinking. I picked it up—a message from Ivana.

Hello, darling. Should I send Watson to pick you up today?

I put the phone back on the bedside and listened. The flat was very silent and still. And it was warm. It was never warm at Marlborough Hall. I stretched luxuriously. It was nice to be back at my own flat. Since being discharged from hospital this was the first time I had spent a night here and I realized that it was probably the best sleep I had had since I could remember. No dreams. No nightmares.

I curled up into the warmth of my sheets and thought about the night before. It was the first time I had gone out on my own. No Daddy, no Ivana, and not even the driver to babysit me. I just called a taxi and went out on my own. It had felt good. And while out I had bumped into Dr. Kane. I hugged the pillow tightly thinking about that look Cookie had interrupted.

Of course, the rest of the night had disintegrated into intolerable boredom, but still nothing could take the glow away from my unexpected brush with Dr. Kane. Cookie spent the whole night talking about people I could not remember and hadn't the least clue about. Every time I shook my head and confessed that I did not remember someone, which was all night, she would raise her voice significantly, as if I was not suffering from amnesia but was stone deaf. 'Oh, but you must remember Pip or Bobo or...'

'I don't remember any of it. I'm sorry,' I said when we parted.

Cookie made a moue with her mouth. 'Think nothing of it. It'll all come back, I'm sure.' And then we parted without agreeing to ever see each other again.

I rolled out of bed and went into the bathroom. I stood in front of the looking glass. My hair was disheveled. I ran my fingers through it and replayed a very special secret: Dr. Kane telling me I have beautiful hair. I never considered my hair beautiful. It was so flyaway that if I did not use half a can of hairspray or tie it back in a ponytail it was always in my face. But he thought it looked like spun gold.

And later he had stared at my mouth. I looked at my mouth, still swollen from sleep, and suddenly I was no longer standing in my bathroom, but somewhere else. Somewhere I did not recognize. It was not like an old photograph, flat, leached of color and fading, but crystal clear, vibrant and real.

I was back in the past—I was remembering!

I saw myself sitting in a plush, red velvet and gilt Louis the XIV armchair, naked but for a pair of shiny black stiletto boots. My hair was long and worn differently and I was wearing false eyelashes. The vision hung in front of me shimmering like a lost city, but so real I could almost reach out and touch it. My heart was racing in my chest. I had remembered a little piece from the past, but it was another piece of the jigsaw.

And then the thought: How could it happen that I was sitting on a red velvet chair naked but for a pair of boots? I ran from the bathroom to my wardrobe to where all my shoes were kept. Some were still in boxes and I opened them all in a rush. But they were just normal shoes, the kind I usually wore. There were no shiny black stiletto boots. I sat back on my heels, confused. Was it really a memory or a figment of my imagination? But it was so real. Had I become confused with the hypnosis? I knelt in front of the open wardrobe. I felt numb and empty. The image of me naked on the red and gilt chair floated into my mind. It was a different me. In a different room. But it was me.

I didn't want to give it up. It was mine. I was ready for my past to return.

I wanted to call Dr. Kane and tell him about the vision, but it was a Saturday and his offices would be closed. Perhaps it was a good thing. I remembered Ivana warning me to be on guard for false memories.

Was it a false memory? *False*.

I stood up and ran to my make-up drawer. I rifled feverishly through the neatly ordered cosmetics in there. I knew it was there. It had to be. And I froze. I found it: a shiver looking for a spine to run up.

A pair of 100% mink false eyelashes.

I opened the purple velour box, ran my thumb along the feathery edge, and I *knew*. The name of this version was Girl You Crazy and I had worn these before. When I was sitting on the red velvet chair. The memory was not false. It was real. What happened to the shiny boots?

I closed my eyes and tried to force the vision back, but the curtain had tumbled down. All the solidity, sound, taste and smell were gone from the vision. It had become just another memory in my head. I felt strangely bereft and a tear rolled down my face. It burned like acid. Beneath the calm and the resignation I was still vanquished and raw. I swallowed hard. I shouldn't cry. Ivana would be so disappointed if she knew that I was indulging in self-pity and hysteria on my first day away from my family.

I remembered the neurosurgeon saying, 'It's all still there. It's not a question of storage, simply one of access. With time... It could come back. Perhaps not all. Most. At least some.'

I wiped my tears away with my hands. Then I went to use the bathroom. After I was dressed I opened the fridge and smiled. Ivana had had it stocked with everything I could possibly want. Milk, orange juice, eggs, bacon, thick slices of good ham, homemade pancakes, bottles of Oxford marmalade and jams bursting with chunky berries. I sat down to a bowl of cereal. I chewed slowly and...relished my solitary state.

After I put away my breakfast things I phoned Ivana. She sounded anxious to have me back in Marlborough Hall. But I was enjoying my sense of freedom after having been in an almost child-like state. It was a nice change from my father treating me as if I was a mental patient that required kid gloves, and my stepbrother and half-sister giving me pitying looks when they thought I wasn't looking.

'I'm fine,' I reassured her, but she made me promise to be home by Wednesday.

After the call I put the phone down and wandered around the flat. I looked in cupboards, touched clothes, books and things that I had acquired and had no memory of. I opened a drawer and found cards—birthday cards from family and friends. An hour passed. I tried to imagine what I did in this flat before the accident and I could not imagine it. Daddy said I did some PR work for the company. But obviously it can't have been an important job as my absence was not being noticed.

And all that time I kept thinking of Dr. Kane and that look that had passed between us. For those few seconds I had not felt cold and numb. I'd felt alive. I knew I had not imagined it. Last night he *wanted* me as much as I wanted him. The clock in the living room chimed. It was nearly time for lunch. Outside it was a fairly decent day and I decided a walk in the brisk air would do me good. So I dressed warmly and left my flat.

By the time I turned into New Bond Street the weather changed somewhat. Dark rain clouds were hovering above. I passed the designer boutiques where Ivana took me shopping when I first got out of hospital. She had impeccable taste and I was so lost and numb I totally left it to her to choose all my clothes and even my perfume. But now that I felt more like my own person I wanted different things.

It was only after I turned left onto Burlington Street and continued down Vigo Street that I consciously realized where I had been going all along. I was on Regent Street when it started to rain. Huge fat drops that fell on my bent head, shoulders, breasts and hands. For a moment I did nothing, just felt them. The coldness.

And then I raised my face up to the drops and let them break on my skin. I opened my mouth and they rained down on my tongue and ran down my throat. I began to laugh. It was the laugh of a mad woman. People who were hurrying under umbrellas turned to stare at me.

I became drenched very quickly. My clothes stuck to me and I shivered with cold as I walked down Shaftesbury Avenue and turned into Rupert Street. Not far to go now. I walked up to the door of Number 34 and rang the bell. Please be in, I prayed.

'Yes?' His voice came through the speaker muffled but recognizable.

'It's Olivia,' I replied.

There was a shocked pause, then the buzzer sounded. The door to his flat was yanked open and he stood framed in the doorway looking down at me. He was wearing a gray T-shirt and faded blue jeans that clung to his hips. His eyes widened when he saw me. I swiped my hand down my hair. Rivulets of water ran down my body. I clenched my teeth to stop them from chattering and walked up the stairs toward him. I knew I must look like a drowned rat.

An expression crossed his face. It could have been anger, frustration or even just plain irritation. 'Come in,' he said and quickly pulled me into his apartment.

Instinctively I tried to snuggle into the wonderful heat of his sturdy form. But he closed the door and letting go of my hand took a step away from me. It was a rejection, pure and simple. But I knew I had not dreamed last night.

'Get out of those and I'll stick them in the dryer. You can have a hot shower in the bathroom. Come, I'll show you where it is.'

He was turning away when my chilled, sluggish muscles reached out and touched his arm. He spun around so quickly it was as if I had burned him. I looked up at him, startled. 'Wait,' I blurted through numb lips.

Our eyes locked.

Like a man in a daze he reached out and his long pianist's fingers traced my jaw gently and caressed my cheek. As if he did not quite believe I was real. I turned my cheek toward the life-giving warmth of his palm.

'Olivia—' He stopped abruptly.

I shivered.

'You shouldn't even be here,' he muttered, shaking his head.

'Why not?' I asked.

'Have your shower and then you have to leave.'

'Why do I have to leave?' I insisted.

'I can't.' He turned away and walked up to a window and stood staring out into the driving rain. His back was rigid with tension.

'Dr. Kane?'

'Have your shower, Olivia. Second door on your right,' he said coldly, without turning around. He did not even want to look at me.

For a few moments there was silence. Then I walked up to him and touched his back. He whirled around, his jaw clenched tight.

'Please—' His voice was tortured.

'I want you.'

The gold went from his eyes. They glowed like wet amber. Wild, ancient, and powerful. Suddenly, as if it was too much to resist, his hand reached out and grabbed a handful of hair from the back of my head. My mouth went dry. I swayed toward him. I could smell him. Soap. Alcohol. *At this time of the afternoon?* And something else. The smells of his day? Impossible to tell. Intriguing nevertheless.

The other hand, rough with urgency, curled around my waist. Hot, solid and possessive. His lips traveled downwards. It must have been only a second but it seemed to take ages. Breathlessly I waited for his lips to find mine. I felt him inhale before our lips touched. And then all hell broke loose and I lost all sense of time or place.

The brutal warmth of his mouth was incredible. All that was cold and lost inside me went up in flames like kindling on a dry night. I laced my fingers through the lushness of his thick hair and moaned. His tongue was fire. Irresistible. A madness that swept along my lower lip. When he bit the edge of my bottom lip hard enough for me to gasp with a mixture of pain and pleasure, his tongue snaked into my open mouth, muscular, cocky, and tasting indescribably delicious.

A rush of heat flared between my legs. I stood on tiptoes like a child reaching for a treat on a high shelf, and sucked the hot and silky flesh like it was toffee. I could have sucked him forever. The greed that flashed inside me was as shocking as the impatience that poured out of me.

I was *starving* for him.

My hands moved of their own volition. Sure, they were very sure. They knew exactly what they were doing. They had done this before. Definitely. With whom I had no idea. But definitely my hands knew what they were doing.

They moved to his belt and unfastened it with an expertise that I could never have expected. His zipper slid down the way it was designed to do. My palm was rubbing his bulging erection through cloth. I felt the massive head of his cock jutting out over the waistband of his underwear. My fingers hooked into the top of his briefs.

Abruptly and with a grunt of dismay he pulled away from my restless hands. Holding me firmly by my upper arms he took a long step back. His eyes were glazed. 'This is fucked up,' he growled harshly. 'I can't do this. It's wrong.'

The magic shattered. My heart started to ache. 'I don't care if it is wrong,' I cried desperately.

'I do. I could damage you, Olivia,' he said harshly.

'So damage me,' I challenged.

He looked at me with anguished eyes. He had vowed to abstain... But how he wanted me. He took another step away and I saw something haunted in his eyes. A raw, bare look. Unbearable hurt. The kind of hurt you never recover from. I recognized it because I had seen the same look in the mirror. All broken pieces and jagged edges. Of a lost soul.

'No,' he said, his voice coarse with lust. 'It's too complicated. You don't understand.'

'I'm not an animal or a suspect to be observed and monitored from afar,' I shouted.

'Don't you think I know that?' he spat at me.

'Fuck me then,' I cried.

At the tone of my voice he changed. As if I had slapped him. As if I had made him remember where he was and what he had been about to do. How close he had come to doing something he would regret. He zipped his jeans. 'You're soaked through. We need to get you into a hot shower,' he said in a brisk, businesslike tone.

It was a rejection. He was rejecting me. I started to shiver, my teeth suddenly chattering.

'Come on,' he said, taking my arm. He took me to his bathroom, where he switched on the shower, and undressed me. I saw his eyes skim over my scars. When I was naked he stood me under the hot spray. The heat was good. I stopped shivering and looked at him through the water running down my eyes. He stared back wordlessly.

'I'm going to leave you now,' he said through clenched teeth. 'There's a bathrobe behind the door. Use it.'

I listened to his footfalls leave the tiled floor and the door closed. I stood in the steam and the heat for a long time, my silent tears mingling with the water. I felt so empty. So lost. I had offered myself to him and he had turned me down. And then I remembered the look in his eyes when they skimmed my scars, and I had to put my palms against the tiles to support my suddenly weak knees.

God! I've been blind. So blind.

11

Marlow

Hearse was playing in the background—bittersweet, gutterfolk songs. *Fireworks* came on and the twanging sound of an electric guitar filled the air. A man's voice sang, *'Gonna be here all night'*.

She stood at the door wrapped up in my bathrobe. She had rolled the sleeves up, but it was way too big for her and it trailed on the floor. Her skin was red, her eyes swollen. We stared at each other. She moved her arm and I glimpsed a curve of pale soft skin.

She was naked under my robe! Music swirled around us. Lust raged inside me. That's what one taste of an obsession does. It makes you a savage. What did she know? Coming here and telling me to go on and damage her. I wanted to open her up and fuck her until she screamed for mercy in that touch-me-not voice of hers. My breath came heavily. *Get a grip.* My fists clenched. This couldn't be about me.

'I've made coffee,' I said.

'Thank you, but no.' Her voice sounded strained.

'Your clothes will be ready soon.'

'What are you hiding, Dr. Kane?'

I froze. That's what you do to dogs in heat. Throw a bucket of cold water. You're left with a boner and no desire. 'What do you mean?' I asked.

'You know some secret about me, don't you?' she accused.

I felt the cold hand of fear for her.

'So it's true,' she cried, her eyes enormous with shock. 'You've found out something about me that you have not allowed me to remember.'

'Listen—'

'How could you? How dare you?' she gasped in disbelief.

'Hang on—' I tried to explain, but she cut me off.

'I trusted you,' she whispered, backing away from me.

I moved toward her and she held up a warding hand.

I halted immediately. 'I was protecting you,' I explained. Even to my own ears it sounded weak.

'Protecting me? From what?' she barked. 'Here's an Americanism you'll understand. Bull-fucking-shit. Just tell me the truth. What is it?' she shouted, her voice now high and hysterical.

'Ask yourself why I would have done something like that,' I said in the most unemotional voice I could reach for.

It stopped her in her tracks, the anger leaving her as suddenly as it had come. She wrapped her arms around herself and frowned with confusion. 'Why?' she asked suspiciously.

'I have nothing to gain from full disclosure, but you have everything to lose. Please, Olivia.'

'Oh God! What is it?' she sobbed slapping her hands to her cheeks. Her knees buckled and she fell to the ground. I strode over to her and carried her to the couch. I lay her on it and put some cushions under her head. She stared up at me fearfully. 'Do my memories have claws?'

'The problem is not insurmountable. I just need a little time to really help you. Will you trust me?'

'I do trust you, Dr. Kane.'

'Thank you, Olivia.'

She worried her lower lip. 'Have I done something really wrong?'

My heart skipped a beat. 'No. You have done *nothing* wrong.'

'Has someone done something bad to me?'

I looked her in the eye. 'It seems that way at the moment.'

'Is that why I can't remember?'

'Maybe. There is no physical reason you cannot remember. Your mind doesn't want you to.'

She frowned. 'If it had happened to you, would you want to remember?'

I thought about the burning car, the smell of them burning, and I smiled sadly. 'No, no, I wouldn't.'

She nodded. 'Something bad happened to you, didn't it?'

'Yes,' I said and fuck me, I felt tears gather at the backs of my eyes. All these years I had never shed a single tear. I had been frozen with horror and now the tears were threatening. I blinked. More in shock than anything else.

She lifted her hand and ran her thumb along my eyelashes, then put her thumb in her mouth. 'I ate your tears,' she said. And she sounded like a child.

Son of a gun, but I think I'm falling for her. I stared incredulously at her, the truth of my situation dawning on me. I was fucking falling for her. Every time we met, a little more. I was already neck deep.

'Yeah, you ate my tears,' I said slowly, as another tear rolled down unchecked.

She lifted her body and, coming close to my face, licked my salty cheek.

The action had an undesirable effect on my body. Like a half-trained polecat my cock reared its ugly head. I tried to move away from her, but she grabbed my forearms with both her hands. I looked down at them, so small and delicate and yet surprisingly strong. I looked up again into her eyes.

'Don't push me away,' she begged.

I closed my eyes. The music had stopped and a thick heavy silence hung between us. All the things I wanted to say and the things buried inside her. She knew me not at all. I wanted to crush her in my arms and keep her next to me forever. I never wanted her to leave. There was such a pleasure in her proximity. To feel her breathe, to touch her soft skin, to smell the clean scent of her hair. I clenched my teeth. 'You have to go. Your clothes must be ready by now.' The words tumbled out of me, harsh and angry.

She went still. Then her hands slipped away from my arm. The music player clicked on again and *Last Mistake* came on.

'While you were sleeping I was drinking,' a man's voice crooned.

I stood up and looked down at her. Her hair was wet and stuck to her head, her nose was red and my old bathrobe was a shapeless blob around her, but she was the most beautiful woman in the world.

'By the way,' she said listlessly, 'Ivana has invited you to stay the weekend at Marlborough Hall. You can bring someone if you like.'

Marlborough Hall

12

Marlow

The fish, even in the fisherman's net, still carries
the smell of the sea.
—Mourid Barghouti

Marlborough Hall had been built for one
purpose and one purpose only—to dazzle. And
to that monumental mission every stone in it
was utterly committed. Its vast mass of
rusticated granite soared, towered, and
sprawled before us as we turned through a
pair of imposing stone piers, topped with
winged bronze chimera.

'Oh my God. Look at that!' Beryl cried as
she dramatically fanned herself with her
hands.

I stopped the Jag and we sat for a moment
looking at the lighted splendor that had been
the seat of the Swanson family for the last
three hundred years. I thought it an
ostentatious fortress and the unfriendliest
place I had ever seen, but when I glanced at
Beryl, I realized she was as horribly enthralled

and fascinated by the naked display of power and wealth, as a rat would be in the face of a striking snake. All I could think of was that somewhere in that hostile pile of stones a pale plant called Olivia was struggling to thrive.

'OK, I'm ready,' Beryl said more calmly.

I started the car and we drove down a wide gravel drive. We crunched to a halt next to an antique Rolls-Royce.

'Isn't this marvelous?' Beryl whispered excitedly.

'That remains to be seen,' I said drily.

'What about the hamper? Do we take it in?' she asked, referring to the hamper of food she had ordered from Fortnum & Mason. She was convinced it was where posh people got their food.

'I'm sure someone will come and collect it together with our overnight bags.'

'Of course, silly me. They have servants, don't they? I hope I don't make a total fool of myself tonight,' Beryl said worriedly.

'You'll be fine. If you get nervous just think of them sitting on the toilet.'

Beryl laughed heartily. 'That's very useful.'

'Shall we?' I asked, my hand on the door handle.

She touched my sleeve. 'Before we go in, I just want to thank you again for asking me to come with you.'

'I couldn't survive it without you, Beryl.'

She beamed with pleasure.

'Come on,' I said, putting a foot out of the car. 'Let's see how the other half live.'

With impeccable timing the massive doors of the house opened and a liveried footman came out to help us. I refused his offer of help with my overnight case, so he made himself useful by carrying Beryl's small suitcase and the hamper.

A man in a butler's uniform complete with spotlessly white gloves politely greeted us in an echoing cold, gray, stone hallway. In a broad Northern accent he informed us that drinks would be served in the Green Saloon in an hour's time. The footman left the hamper on a stand nearby and led us down a short walkway hung with large tapestries toward a gargantuan, double-storied chamber. It had a balustraded gallery around all four sides and its walls were lined with full-length portraits of the family, no doubt executed by the great masters.

'Goodness me, I feel quite touched by the golden wand,' Beryl said in a stage whisper. Her eyes were wide.

'Hmmm...'

We followed the footman up a grand marble staircase with a red runner carpet, and down a narrow corridor. He stopped outside a door and respectfully said, 'Here we are.'

He opened it, and upon entering the room, stood back to allow us to fully appreciate our lodgings. It was a large paneled room that had been prepared for our arrival. The lamps were lit, there was a fire roaring in the fireplace and a vase with flowers on a table. It smelt of fresh linen. And on the antique, canopied four-poster bed, towels and bars of soap were laid out.

'Breakfast will be served from seven until nine, or if you prefer you can ring for it to be brought up.'

Then he opened another door, which revealed a connecting door. He opened that door and Beryl stepped into the room that she had been assigned.

After he had gone Beryl knocked on the connecting door.

'Come in,' I called.

'Isn't this amazing? Can you believe people actually live like this?' she asked and sank onto the green brocade sofa.

'It is an unfair world we live in,' I said mildly and disappeared into the bathroom.

When I came out with the tooth glass Beryl jumped up.

'Oh good. A dressing drink? I'll have one too,' she said and went off into her room then returned with her tooth glass. I opened my bag and poured us both a healthy slug of whiskey. Beryl didn't stay long. She wanted to look her best for dinner. I sat on my own watching the logs in the fire burn. Evening fell and brought with it a sense of timelessness. I merged into it together with all those people who had lived there before.

I was feeling mellow and peaceful and could have sat there with only me for company when Beryl knocked on the door forty minutes later.

'What do you think? Is it too little or too much?' she asked.

She was wearing a long blue dress that had a slight shimmer to it and a sunburst necklace with matching colored stones. I knew she bought them especially for that night. I smiled, feeling a great burst of tenderness for her. 'You look lovely.'

'You really mean it?'

'Have you ever known me to say something I didn't mean?'

'That's true.'

I pulled myself out of my chair and shrugged into the jacket I arrived in.

'Aren't you going to dress for dinner?'

'Nope.'

'You'll be the only one.'

'So?'

She widened her eyes. 'OK, boss.'

13

Marlow

'They don't spend much on heating, do they?' Beryl said with a shiver as we walked along the freezing corridor.

To access the Green Saloon we had to cross the Marble Room. A large room filled with fine French furniture, precious carpets from the Middle East and stuffed full with priceless works of art. It gave the impression of unrivaled luxury, but once again I had the distinct impression that the house was stalked by a frightening loneliness.

A footman—not the one from earlier—held open a set of tall double doors and ushered us into the Green Saloon. It was another opulent room with more works of art and expensive antiques, but it was much warmer here. A waiter stepped forward and asked us what we wanted to drink. Beryl ordered a glass of white wine and I asked for an American size double measure of Jack Daniel's. The British idea of a double is laughable.

'Right away, sir,' he said crisply and disappeared.

There were about twelve to fifteen people milling around, talking in small groups, but at our entrance almost everyone stopped talking, and was either openly or surreptitiously sizing us up. Maybe I'd had more whiskey than I had intended, but all the men appeared to have been dressed by the same tailor.

Almost immediately my gaze tangled with Olivia's. She was conversing with a middle-aged couple, but she threw a shy smile in my direction. I nodded and looked away, and my eyes fell upon our hostess. Lady Swanson was standing by the super-large marble fireplace listening attentively to a tall, balding man. As I watched she broke away and came toward us, smiling as if seeing us was a dream come true.

'Hello, how terribly sweet of you to come all the way from London,' she trilled.

'It was kind of you to ask us, Lady Swanson.' I nodded toward Beryl. 'This is Beryl Baker, my assistant.'

She smiled charmingly. 'But of course, I remember you.'

'You have *such* a beautiful home,' Beryl gushed.

'Yes,' she said with a little laugh, 'we rather like it, but it can be frightfully dreary down here, you know. No proper restaurants or theaters and freezing pipes all winter.'

'I wouldn't mind. It's *so* beautiful,' Beryl said. Her little face was quite red with excitement. 'Oh, and thank you *so* much for inviting me.'

'Not at all. I'm delighted to have you both here.' Lady Swanson leaned forward, her eyes sparkling as if she was excluding the rest of the room, and sharing an intimate secret that only Beryl and I were privy to. She was a socially expert individual of the highest order, obviously. 'Was there a lot of Friday traffic on the roads?'

'No. It was fine,' I said, hiding my amusement.

Beryl was still nodding vigorously in agreement when I cast my eye out for the waiter. He was walking toward me with a straight back and a tray with a glass of wine and my whiskey placed on a napkin square.

Beryl and I accepted our drinks and Lady Swanson said, 'You must let me introduce you to my husband.'

We followed her toward a large, gilded grandfather clock where a rotund, balding, florid-faced man was standing stiffly next to a stout woman with a pink face, fat, heavily bejeweled hands, and a snooty tilt to her nose. Her lipstick had bled into the leathery creases around her mouth.

'Darling,' Lady Swanson said, 'this is Dr. Kane, the hypnotherapist I was telling you about. The one that's treating Vivi.' She turned to me. 'Dr. Marlow Kane, my husband, Lord William Elliot Swanson.'

So that was little Olivia's nickname—Vivi. Totally unsuitable.

'Ah,' he said, his bushy gray eyebrows raised, as he took my hand and pumped it heartily. I could imagine him in a waxed jacket, gun in hand, whistling for his dogs.

'Hello,' I said, and listened while Lady Swanson introduced the woman with the greasy lipstick. She had a double-barreled last name that I did not bother to remember. She looked at me vaguely—a subtle method of telling me I belonged to an inferior class.

'And this is Beryl Baker, his assistant,' Lady Swanson said. With that piece of information the woman's eyes completely glassed over.

At that point the butler caught Lady Swanson's eye. She nodded and excused herself. Lord Swanson nodded blankly at Beryl and turned to me. 'Did you have much trouble getting here?'

I sighed inwardly. 'No. It was fine.'

'No traffic? Don't people leave London like lemmings at the weekend?' he boomed.

'Not this weekend.'

'Jolly good.'

And with that the conversation was apparently over. He smiled at us in an expansive if dim way, and nodded us away.

I steered Beryl away. Olivia's father was dull and not particularly bright, but his birthright as the male heir of the Swanson fortune meant that he was deferred to so sycophantically that he had no idea how uninteresting and stupid he really was. All these people who bowed and behaved as if the sun shone out of his ass were happy to go along with the illusion of his greatness because it kept their importance in the scheme of things secure.

We were drifting toward the tall, mullioned windows when a familiar voice said, 'Hello. So glad you could make it.'

We turned around to face Olivia. She was wearing a velvet black dress with a high neckline and black lace sleeves. Her glossy hair was up in some sort of chignon that made me imagine taking it down and twisting it around my fist as I rammed into her.

'Hi,' Beryl grinned.

'I see you've met Daddy,' she said softly, her silvery eyes straying from me to Beryl.

'Yes. He seems...very nice,' Beryl said.

Olivia's expression said that she did not believe Beryl thought any such thing, but all she said was, 'I'd like you both to meet my siblings.'

First was her sister, Lady Daphne.

She had inherited her mother's beautiful eyes and she had very good skin. Otherwise she was, unfortunately, the spitting image of her father. She was only nineteen, but incredibly, she had already cultivated the critical, calculating hauteur of a dowager. Her voice was a sarcastic, assessing drawl and her cold gaze dismissed and traveled away from us even as she said, 'How do you do?'

An awkward silence ensued as soon as the introductions were done. Olivia quickly herded us away and introduced us to a sleek man standing next to a painting of a dour ancestor, his eyes glazed with boredom. He was wearing a double-breasted, navy wool pinstripe suit, the pocket square, stuffed not folded, and the tie a different pattern but still working together perfectly. The tie knot was a gentleman's knot, small, tight, four-in-hand with a dimple. Obviously a polo playing, champagne guzzling city boy.

Beryl said something quietly in Olivia's ear and both ladies excused themselves. I presumed they were on their way to the powder room. My eyes nearly swiveled around to turn and watch her go.

'So you're the hypnotist?' Jacobi Gough Swanson drawled, eyeing me curiously over the rim of his champagne glass.

'I'm afraid so.'

'Mummy seems to think you're rather wonderful.'

'It's not certain that will be her deathbed opinion yet.'

'I have no doubt you'll do very well,' he said suavely, but some quickly hidden expression in his eyes made me wonder if Olivia had a secret enemy in him.

'I don't suppose you hunt?' he asked.

'As a matter of fact, I do.' *But not foxes*, I added in my head.

His lips twitched unpleasantly. 'Good. You can join us tomorrow.'

'Thank you, but we'll be leaving right after breakfast.'

'Perhaps next time.'

'Sure, why not.'

'So what's it like being a hypnotist?' There was a smug chuckle in his voice.

'Not much different from selling hundred-year Mexican government bonds denominated in euros, or ten-year Swiss bonds at negative yields, I suppose,' I said quietly.

His eyes narrowed. I had just pulled his superiority rug out from under his feet.

'Does that mean it's not going well with Olivia?' he asked coldly.

I looked him squarely in the eye. 'Olivia's case is complicated. Not that I am at liberty to discuss it with you.'

He appeared suddenly amused. 'Is that code for my sister's bonkers?'

So he was jealous of his stepsister. 'No. It could be code for don't believe all you are told.'

He widened his eyes sarcastically. 'What fun! A mystery.'

I refused to be baited. I smiled coldly. I knew his type. He was an unpleasant, selfish, spoilt brat, and I didn't like him, so it was weird that it was he who should then give me the biggest clue of all to solving the mystery that was Olivia.

'Do you think she's making it all up?' he asked.

'Why would you think that?'

'Well, it's a bit careless to lose one's memory twice in one's lifetime, wouldn't you say?'

I frowned. 'What are you talking about?'

'Didn't anybody tell you?' he sneered triumphantly. 'The first time my sister lost her memory was when she was five years old.'

Alarm was crawling in my belly. 'Under what circumstances?'

'She fell down the stairs, hit her head, and completely trashed five years worth of memories. Had to start from scratch. Of course, I know only the barest facts. I was only three.' He delivered his speech with an aloof, deadpan expression, his mouth hardly moving, keeping his upper lip very stiff.

I stared at him, shocked. Why had no one told me?

'Are you familiar with the effects of closed head injuries?' he asked cordially, as if he was asking if I had read the weather report for tomorrow.

I nodded curtly. Depression, personality changes and psychiatric issues.

14

Marlow

More rattled than I wanted to admit, I glanced away from him and saw Olivia and Beryl returning.

'We'll be having dinner in a minute,' Olivia said. 'And Ivana was wondering if you'd like to take Lady Calthrope in.' I followed her glance to a tight-lipped, bone-thin woman in her mid-sixties seated on one of the sofas.

'Of course,' I said, just as dinner was announced.

I walked over to Lady Calthrope and she looked up at me with pale, hooded eyes. 'Are you taking me in?' she demanded.

'Unless you don't want me to,' I said.

She raised a thin, blue-veined hand imperiously. I grasped it and helped her up. She stood for a moment staring boldly at me. 'So you're the American hypnotist.'

'Yes.'

She linked her hand through my arm and without the least trace of embarrassment said,

'That's good. I was rather afraid you might be one of those *ghastly* Americans.'

There was nothing to say to that so arm in arm we followed the tasteful procession in to dinner. The State Dining Room was everything a State Room should be: blended strawberries wallpaper, seventeenth-century ceiling murals, a dining table that spanned from one end of the room to the other, massive chandeliers, heavy gilt mirrors, museum-size paintings, and a stunningly carved marble fireplace. We took our seats amid the flowers and candelabras.

I looked for the waiter and nodded at him. He returned speedily with my American measure of whiskey.

I had Lady Calthrope on my left, which, according to etiquette, meant that I was to talk to her until the first course was cleared away. There was no sharing platitudes with her—it was more like bouts of blunt trauma with an eccentric twist. Between rounds I glanced at Beryl and she smiled or raised her eyebrows at me from across the table, but I quickly realized that she was sitting next to a man who had decided that no conversation at all was possible with her. After a few failed attempts to engage him, poor Beryl was spooning her buttery leek and Stilton soup in stony silence.

Although I was intensely aware of Olivia sitting three guests away on my left, I never let my gaze travel to her. When the places were cleared, as custom required, I turned to converse with the guest on my right.

The Baroness Wentworth was a straight-backed woman with sharp blue eyes and pale lipstick. She smiled mildly at me. 'So, you're a hypnotist.'

'Yes,' I said politely, and catching the waiter's eyes, nodded.

She glanced sideways at me. 'Is it dangerous to look you in the eye?'

'I wouldn't recommend it,' I said gravely.

She giggled. 'You don't mean to say those frightful stage hypnotists are fakes?'

I shrugged. 'It depends. If you see inconsistencies, then it's a fakery. If you don't, it isn't.'

'Inconsistencies such as?'

'If a hypnotized person picks up a glass of water that he has been told is battery acid and drinks it then he is not hypnotized. He is either pretending or a shill. If he refuses to drink it then he is, because he genuinely believes it is battery acid and it will harm him.'

She turned fully toward me. 'How fascinating. And how does one become a hypnotist?'

'I wasn't always a hypnotist. I began as a neurologist.'

'I like clever people and I've always made a beeline for them.'

I glanced at Beryl. She was now being ignored by the gentleman on her other side.

Her shoulders were sodden with disappointment and humiliation. All around me bits of foreign conversation swirled. An old boy was talking about getting pissed in the Bullingdon Club, a woman had been served a nice fat red Margaux at lunch the day before, someone else was discussing his stock of rare breeds in his organic farm, another had spent fifty thousand pounds at an auction but could not remember what he bought. The hubris and rudeness of this group of people was just too much.

Beryl was a sweet person who had arrived in such high spirits, so excited to be in the presence of the 'cream of society'. But the haves had thoroughly snubbed a have-not. I was furious on her behalf and I was damned if I would let these stuck-up bores treat her as if she was a non-person.

I picked up my glass and to the open-mouthed horror of the Baroness I excused myself, and, standing up, sauntered over to where Beryl was sitting. The entire table had fallen silent with shock.

I looked at the man on Beryl's right. 'I'd like to exchange places with you. I believe I'm offering a far more advantageous seating choice. You'll be sitting next to a Baroness no less.'

There was a horrified gasp from one of the ladies on my left.

The man gaped like a caught fish. He looked around him and then incredulously at me.

'Surely you don't mean for me to move halfway through dinner?' he asked as if doing so would be tantamount to committing a cardinal sin.

My eyes and jaw were answer enough.

Without another word and with stony-eyed resentment he pushed his chair back and walked around to my seat. I took his place and winked at Beryl. 'I thought you looked a bit lonely,' I said.

She grinned suddenly, her whole face lighting up. Around us servants were busy moving plates and cutlery to accommodate the switch.

I glanced up to catch the waiter's eye and met Olivia's eyes instead. For a second we stared at each other then I moved my gaze along and met Ivana's regard. Her expression was carefully veiled. Only a mask of social politeness was on display. She raised her eyebrows slightly at me. It was impossible to say what she intended to convey with this subtle gesture.

After dinner the men and the women separated as if we were still stuck in Edwardian times. Without the sexual tension provided by Olivia or the warmth of Beryl I became quickly and intolerably bored. I consumed another dose of Lord Swanson's fine Scotch and left. I couldn't stand the smell of their cigars or their unsubtle attempts to turn me into an outsider by constantly referring to the charmed circle of people they all knew. I was an outsider. God, was I glad that I wasn't a member of their exclusive club.

I made my way back to my room. Someone had come in, drawn the curtains, and added fresh logs to the fire. It looked cozy, but it was actually chilly. There was a distinct draft coming from somewhere. I retrieved the tooth glass from the bathroom and poured myself a glass of whiskey. I drank it by the fire staring at the dancing orange flames and considered the events of the evening.

What her brother told me put a whole different slant onto Olivia's amnesia. I had to get to the bottom of it soon. There was very little time left before Olivia was going to insist on knowing exactly what was going on.

I felt the drink seep into my brain cells, relaxing me. I was starting to feel drowsy when there was a knock on my door. Surprised, I went to open it.

Young, haughty, dismissive, precocious Daphne was standing in the deserted corridor. I raised my eyebrows. She was the last person I expected to see outside my door. She had been such a bitch. 'All well?' I asked.

'Can I come in?'

'Sure,' I said, opening the door wider.

She sailed in. I closed the door and leaned against it.

'Dinner was pretty filthy,' she said with her back to me.

'I thought it was excellent.'

She swung around on one heel, like a dancer. 'Are you sleeping with her?'

'Whom did you have in mind?' I straightened away from the door, my face expressionless.

'My half-sister, of course,' she replied, with a pleasant smile.

And I knew then without a shadow of a doubt that she hated Olivia with the fierce hatred that comes from excruciating envy.

I crossed my arms. 'Not that it's any of your business, but no.'

She smiled shyly, but her eyes were filled with malicious delight. 'I saw her watching you.'

'I don't make a habit of sleeping with my clients. Far too confusing for me, let alone them.'

She smiled again, this time in that cold, aloof manner of hers. 'What about their sisters? Have you slept with any of them?'

I stared at her. She was totally different from the girl/woman I had met in the Green Saloon. This was the Daphne Swanson with her well-bred spine exposed, without the pretensions or the aura of fake hauteur that her social set deliberately cultivated to place them apart from mere mortals. Here was the real Daphne, the central figure in her own drama.

'I can't say I have,' I said mildly.

She bit her lower lip. 'Would it be too awful to start tonight?'

My eyebrows shot up, but before I could answer there was another knock on my door.

She blanched, but in a flash she ran into one of the cupboards and shut the door on herself.

Bemused, I opened the door. Beryl was standing outside. Her cheeks were flushed and she looked glazed about the eyes. Why, she was as drunk as a skunk.

'Oh good, you're still awake,' she slurred. 'I was hoping you'd be.' She proceeded to sway unsteadily into the middle of the room right where Daphne had been standing. She turned around and almost lost her balance.

'Are you all right?'

She waved her hand and smiled benevolently. 'I feel great. I just wanted to thank you for what you did tonight at the dinner table.' She raised her forefinger and wagged it at me. 'You rescued me.'

'It was nothing,' I said quickly.

'No, no, no,' she argued shaking her head. 'No one else would have done such a thing. You're a good man, Dr. Kane. A really good man. And handsome, too. You're really handsome, you know. If I was twenty years younger...'

I looked at her with amusement. She was going to be mortified in the morning. If she remembered, that is.

'It's a lucky woman who gets you,' she continued.

I shifted away from the door. 'Where have you been all this while?' I found it hard to believe she had been accepted into the club and had been getting sloshed with them all this time.

She grinned happily. 'You'll never believe it, but I found out that the cook is from the same little village in Devon that I'm from. Fancy that! I've been in the kitchen having a good old chinwag with her all this while. It was fun. She's so nice. She opened a bottle of sloe berry vodka that she made herself and we had a few glasses. Phew! Potent stuff.'

'I can see that.'

'Right. The floor keeps tilting. I guess I ought to go to bed.'

I went to my bag and pushed out two tabs of headache tablets and dropped them into her palm. 'Life won't be worth it tomorrow morning if you don't take these right away.'

She smiled dreamily. 'You really are such a Prince Charming.'

I opened the connecting door.

'See you at breakfast,' she said and stumbled through the open doorway. I closed it and the cupboard door opened.

Daphne stepped out coolly as if hiding in cupboards was a thing she did every day. She walked up to me. 'She's quite right. You are quite the prince,' she said, unzipping her dress and letting it slide to the floor. In that chilly room she stood as naked as the day she was born. I'll admit she had a good body, a very good body.

She curved one corner of her lip invitingly and very deliberately began to walk toward me. I had the impression she could have been a good lay. Energetic and probably insatiable, but there was something viperish about her that made me think I'd live to regret any time spent in her pussy.

How did one politely reject a Sloane Ranger with a trust fund in the Bahamas? A vindictive one at that. Thankfully, I didn't have to. There was a knock on the door and Lady Daphne became a flash of pale skin as she raced to her dress, picked it up and returned to the cupboard.

This was fast becoming a comical farce. I opened the door and Olivia was standing there in her coat.

She smiled. 'Get your jacket on and come with me. I want to show you something.'

'You make it sound dangerous,' I said.

'I'll keep you safe,' she said, with a smile.

'Ah, but who will keep you safe?'

She blushed and I realized that I must have drunk far more than I thought. I was flirting with her! Every sober cell in my brain knew I shouldn't go with her. It wasn't prudent. But the alcohol was suddenly racing powerfully in my veins. I was surrounded by that horrid smell of her perfume that had actually started to grow on me and I fucking *wanted* to be with her.

Oh fuck it.

15

Marlow

I pulled my jacket from the sofa back and shrugging into the coat went out into the corridor to Olivia. A few steps down the corridor I turned to her.

'Can you hang on here for just a sec? Got to sort something out. I'll be real fast.'

'All right,' she said, looking up at me with soft eyes.

I turned around and went back into my room. There was no polite way to do this. I closed the door, strode to my wardrobe and yanked it open abruptly. Daphne was standing inside clutching her dress against her body. She blinked up at me in surprise. Exactly the reaction I had hoped to achieve—disorientate her conscious mind. I reached in and took her left wrist in my right hand.

'Keep your arm soft,' I instructed, fixing my eyes on hers.

Taken by surprise she obliged immediately. I raised my other hand higher than her eye level so her confused eyes would automatically have to follow, and travel upwards. Smoothly I moved my hand toward her face knowing it would cause her to instinctively sway back slightly, an action that should have also brought on a mild sensation of dizziness.

It happened quickly after that.

My hand reached her forehead and I began to stroke it, creating both bewilderment and a rush of feel-good serotonin into her brain. As her eyeballs began to invert, I firmly issued the order, 'Sleep.'

Her head lolled back just as I curled one hand around the back of her neck while my other caught her limp body as it slid downwards. Carefully, I leaned her against the back of the cupboard.

When you see those TV evangelists dropping people in waves, this together with sleight of hand is the procedure they are employing. Called the rapid induction method it can be done with an arm pull, a handshake, or even by just following the hand movements of an expert stage hypnotist. The effects are impressive, but they don't last long. They were, however, sufficient for my needs.

'Can you hear me, Daphne?' I asked.

She nodded slowly.

'Good. You will remain standing solidly on your feet for one minute. Then you will wake up feeling sleepy, get dressed, and immediately go to your room where you will fall into a deep and restful sleep. You will not ever remember being here or conversing with me.'

I left the cupboard doors open and went out of the room to join Olivia in the corridor.

'Ready?' she whispered.

'Yeah, ready.' A thrill of excitement coursed through my veins. We were both castaway people on a midnight adventure.

Silently we journeyed through deserted corridors and down an uncarpeted, wooden staircase at the back, which, I assumed, must be the servants' staircase. We passed bare walls and uncarpeted tiles, a stark difference to the opulence and luxury we had come from. Then we crossed a large kitchen, dark and still and very clean, and then we were out into the night air. A cold wind blew at us. We rounded the corner and we were at the side of a large Victorian conservatory.

She turned around to me, her eyes shining in the dark. 'We could have gone in through the house, but I much prefer this entrance.'

She opened the door and we entered the most beautiful garden I had ever seen. I mean, I'm not into plants in any shape or form, but this one had to be seen. Milky moonlight was flooding in through the windows and turning the interior into a hauntingly beautiful garden.

In fact, I had the impression of a secret forest. There must have been hundreds of plants in there—they grew up the walls, hung from the ceilings and covered all available spaces that had not been designated as paths for walking on or a small patch where there was a small metal table and a canopied swing seat. Ferns tickled my legs.

I rubbed my hands together. It was actually warm in there, the atmosphere a little bit foggy and redolent with the smell of earth moss. The gentle sound of water dripping was soothing.

She flicked a light switch and clusters of round white lamps came on and threw their diffused light on the plants, walls, the geometrically patterned floor and on her beautiful face.

'Isn't it perfect?'

'Yes. It reminds me of a place of worship, like a chapel—cool, dark, quiet.'

She looked at me, surprised. 'You go to church?'

'I was an altar boy when I was a kid, but I've given up God.'

'What happened?'

I didn't tell her about my children screaming, then burning to their deaths just yards away from me, about the little shoe that dropped close to me as if straight from the sky.

'The real truth is,' I said carefully, 'I could not have resisted Christianity if the story had ended with, "Why hast thou forsaken me?" But the happy ending made it less interesting.'

She frowned. 'That's rather morbid.'

'You think so?' I shrugged. 'It's the real condition of humanity. Our lives are ones of pure abandonment. Somewhere trampling through the universe are trillions of unanswered prayers still looking for God.'

She touched the edge of a green ceramic pot and ran her finger, the nail pearlescent in the glow from the lamps, along the ridge. 'I like the idea of God. Someone to turn to when things get really bad.'

'Yeah, it's a nice thought,' I conceded.

'But it was this place that saved me. When I first came out of hospital I was like a caged creature. Every day I paced the confines of my cage and came upon bars in exactly the same place, and unable to realize why I could go no farther.'

She looked around her.

'But one day Ivana wheeled me in here and I found it so peaceful and soothing that I wanted to spend more and more time here. And then I began to realize that I could make it more beautiful. There were not so many plants here then and I set about redesigning everything. Now this is where I spend most of my time. When you have your hands in dirt you don't think. You become a part of the earth.'

I stared at her. God! She was heartbreakingly beautiful. Her little face lit up about a bunch of plants. It was impossible to imagine her in a sex club. I remembered the heady, drug-like feel and the taste of her. And how fantastically our bodies had come together and lust boiled my blood. I was on dangerous ground. Very dangerous ground. What the hell was I thinking of coming here alone with her?

'It's just a little thing,' she was saying softly, totally unaware of how she was affecting me, 'but it makes me happy and I wanted you to see it.' She clasped her arms, like a child waiting for my approval.

Hell, Lady Olivia, my approval was a done deal from the moment you walked into my office.

I knew I should get out of that place. It was too closed. Here she was too much of a temptation. I had a fantasy about her. I wanted to see my cock in her mouth. In my fantasy she struggled to fit it all in. I felt my body start heating up. I needed to get the fuck out now. This was where the rubber met the road.

'Thanks for showing it to me. It's beautiful. But I should get back.'

'Wait,' she cried softly, and took my hand.

She pulled me to a pool. Goldfish swam in pale circles.

'Daphne says it's a bit bourgeois to have fish, but I like them.' She bent down to lean against the pool's edge and her dress seemed stretched around her boyish hips. Unwanted thoughts of my cock slowly disappearing into her body rushed into my mind. Without any warning my erection bulged painfully against my zipper. Fuck. This was nuts. I was venturing into impossible territory. I wanted her so bad she was going to smell it on my breath.

I needed to get back to my room, like now. Blissfully unaware of what was going on in my mind and body she pointed to some cast iron columns.

'See that there? That is a Victorian rainwater collection system. It's really clever. It diverts the water from the glass roof into an underground storage tank.'

I stared at the columns feeling almost overwhelmed by the force of my desire for her.

'I should go.' My voice sounded thick and strained.

'Why?'

I looked at her beautiful face, with its large, shining eyes upturned to me, and that delicious mouth slightly parted.

'I think we both know it's for the best.'

'Why is it?'

'We've been through this before, but it would also be very unprofessional of me to become partial.'

'Is that the only reason?'

I sighed heavily.

'But you want to...' She let her voice trail.

I felt suddenly angry. 'For fuck's sake, Olivia, what the hell do you want from me? I'm holding on by my fingernails here.'

She smiled, a shy, pleased quirk to her mouth. 'I'm glad to hear that.'

'Goodnight, Olivia.'

'Dr. Kane?'

'Yeah?'

'I thought you were impeccably uncivil at the dinner table.'

I jammed my fists into my trouser pockets. 'Ah, the Beryl episode.'

'Of course, you realize you'll never be invited back again,' she said with a smile.

'Oh bugger.'

She giggled. 'It sounds funny when you say it.'

'Sleep well, Olivia.'

'Goodnight, Dr. Kane.'

I turned around and left her among her plants. A mysterious nymph who would haunt my dreams that night.

16

Olivia

My sister telephoned. 'Shall we go for some cold fish?' she asked.

I laughed, happy those words sounded familiar. They had come from behind the veil. I did not know in what context, when or where she had said them to me before, but I knew she had. That was how she described Japanese food. 'Why? Are you on a diet?' I asked.

'A bit,' she admitted.

We agreed to meet for lunch at Nobo in Mayfair.

I arrived early so I ordered a glass of pale cream sherry and waited for her upstairs. She breezed in looking very Sloaney in a vintage Hardy Amis pantsuit and camel hair coat. I smiled and gave a little wave as she approached.

'Traffic was a nightmare,' she complained as she plonked down her Gucci tote, took off her coat and dropped it carelessly on the seat next to me. Elegantly she eased herself into our banquette and turned to me with a flick of her head. 'You look well. Are you off somewhere nice?'

'No, I'm going home after this.'

She lifted a languid finger at a passing waiter and he made for her, smiling. He obviously knew her.

'I'll have whatever she's having,' she told him and he disappeared with a deferential nod. That was the thing about my half-sister. She was like her mother—no matter where she went, she immediately and effortlessly commanded fawning respect. She was so different when I first met her after my amnesia it surprised me we even shared the same gene pool.

I took a sip of my drink. When she turned toward me, I said, 'I saw Maurice the other day.' Maurice was a friend of hers.

'Really? Where?'

'At the butcher.'

'How is he?'

'Still reeling from his divorce, I dare say. He asked after you.'

'Did he? I wonder why. He's a blithering idiot,' she dismissed callously.

The waiter came with her glass of sherry and we placed our orders.

She turned to me resolutely. 'So how are the sessions with the hypnotist coming on?'

I shrugged. 'All right, I suppose.'

'What on earth does that mean? Have you or haven't you remembered anything yet?'

I shifted uncomfortably. 'A bit.'

She raised her eyebrows. 'What, exactly?'

'Well, I remembered a few occasions. The birthday party when I was five, my mother telling Daddy she had cancer. Oh and I remembered finding Jacobi in bed at fifteen with his hardcore German transsexual magazines.'

We grinned at each other.

'Well,' she said with a mischievous look. 'He's a screaming transvestite now.'

'What?' I exclaimed.

'Yes,' she confirmed briefly and suddenly changed the subject. 'What else have you remembered?'

'The other memories are unimportant little pieces of the big puzzle.'

'That's it? Unimportant little pieces of the big puzzle. At his prices?'

I colored. 'We are making progress, but Dr. Kane is cautious so there is no question of false memories occurring.'

She stared at me. 'I can't imagine there are any buried memories, can you?'

'I don't know. I do have the odd unsettling dream.'

'What kind of unsettling dream?'

I bit my lip. 'Just strange things that don't make sense.'

She laughed. 'Dreams are not supposed to make sense. You should see what mine are like. That's no excuse for dragging out your...treatment.'

That tiny pause was meant to tell me she did not think much of my treatment. 'He's not dragging out my treatment. He's just being cautious. He thinks I could be damaged if the process is not done properly.'

She looked at me in a non-committal way. 'Like what happened to his wife?'

He was married! I gazed at her in shock. 'His wife?' I croaked, feeling such a fool.

She leaned forward, her eyes shining with some emotion that I could not figure out. 'Yes, didn't you know? She committed suicide in the most horrendous way. Locked herself inside her car in a Starbucks car park with their two children and a few gas tanks and pulled the pin off a grenade. From what I understand the children were just babies.'

The world tilted to an unnatural angle and my mouth dropped open with horror. 'What?'

At that moment the food arrived and Daphne transferred her attention from me to the two waitresses who were standing by us.

I shut my mouth with a snap. My order of rock shrimp tempura was carefully placed in front of me, and a platter of iced Kumamoto oysters topped with caviar, and a trio of Nobu sauces on the side, was set in front of Daphne. I stared at my food blankly. When I raised my head Daphne was smiling at me.

'Did you remember that you always have the tempura here?' she asked.

Again I felt the rug pulled out from under my feet. I had no memory of ever ordering tempura. In fact, I couldn't remember ever coming to this restaurant. 'Did I?' I asked.

'Yes, always,' she confirmed gaily as she picked up an oyster, expertly detached it from its shell, and delicately swallowed it. She pulled a face. 'The caviar is not very good.'

I picked up my knife and fork in an effort to be casual. 'Daphne, you were telling me about Dr. Kane.'

'Yes, it was a terrific shame. He had to leave the States in disgrace. Completely ruined his career.'

'Why?' I whispered.

'I gather she had planned it so he would see them all burn. Eye witnesses said she looked directly at him and smiled.' She shuddered. 'It was one of those revenge suicides.'

'How absolutely awful.'

She helped herself to another oyster. 'Yes, ghastly. Especially when you take into account that he had treated her with some experimental new method he pioneered and helped her recover memories of childhood sexual abuse.' She dabbed her mouth and took a slow sip of wine. 'I expect he had ruined her and she hated him and wanted him to know that he had. And she took the children with her so he wouldn't be able to do the same with them.'

My mind went blank with dismay. 'How absolutely awful,' I repeated stupidly.

'Probably why he wants to take it slow with you. He's afraid that history might repeat itself.'

I leaned back, my appetite gone, and looked through the full-height windows at Hyde Park. 'I'm not suicidal.' I brought my gaze back to her. 'Am I?'

She laughed, carefree as a bird, and picked up another oyster. 'Obviously not, silly. But from his point of view—once bitten, twice shy, and all that. I'd be careful, all the same, that you don't go falling for him. He is attractive.' She paused with a conspiratorial half-smile. 'In an obvious, common sort of way, I suppose.' The mollusc slipped noiselessly down her throat.

The remark was so catty it took my breath away and the rest of the meal passed in a daze of gossip about people we knew. I answered all her questions automatically or nodded and shook my head where appropriate.

The black cod marinated in sweet miso sauce arrived soon after and I consumed it without tasting it. I watched Daphne delicately nibble at razored vegetables and chow down Nobo's signature dish, yellowtail sashimi fired with a slice of jalapeño in yuzu dressing.

A waiter tried to get us to look at the dessert menu.

'I couldn't do pudding, but I wouldn't mind the Suntory whiskey cappuccino,' Daphne said sweetly.

I picked up the bill and then we were outside kissing.

The valet brought her car around and handed her the keys with impressive sucking up. She passed him a ten-pound note. He seemed happy with it.

'Do you need a ride to your flat?' she asked.

I shook my head. 'It's a lovely day. I'd like to walk for a bit before I go back.'

We kissed each other quickly on both cheeks.

'Cheer up, darling. It might never happen.'

I smiled weakly.

'Will you be home for the weekend?' By home she meant Marlborough Hall. Even though we both had apartments in London and spent more time there, we never referred to them as home. Only Marlborough Hall was ever called home.

'Yes, I suppose I will,' I said quietly.

'Well, I'm off. See you at the weekend,' she called and slipped jauntily into the driver's seat of her Audi. I watched her drive away before I set off on my walk.

It was a cold, crisp day and I turned my collar up and walked past the car showroom. They had a bright yellow Lamborghini in the window. I walked down Park Lane, crossed the road, and entered the park.

The afternoon sun had come out from behind the clouds. The blades of grass looked as clear-cut and bright as jewels. I strolled to a bench and sat down. The park was peaceful

with only a few people hurrying along the path. I looked at the bare trees waiting for spring to clothe them again, and sensed inside me a puzzled wonder.

Why exactly was I so troubled by what Daphne had revealed?

And then I knew. It pained me to think of him suffering. More than anything else, I couldn't bear the thought of him in distress. The sun dipped behind thick clouds again and the temperature began to drop fast.

I stood and left the park, now filled with lengthening shadows. I made a wide circuit round it and came out of the screen of fluted Ionic columns of Aspley Gate. As I hurried away the last rays of the weak evening sun flared briefly on the windows of the Hilton across the road. Then it was gone. I clutched the edges of my coat, and carried on past Green Park Tube station. Up ahead I crossed the street and entered the Ritz.

The heat inside brought a delicious languor to my frozen limbs.

Shaking my fingers to bring some warmth back into them I went up to the concierge's station. 'Hello,' I said. 'I'm afraid I don't have a booking but...'

'Lady Olivia,' he greeted so loudly and obsequiously that people turned to look. 'But of course we have a table for you.'

He signaled to a passing waiter who escorted me into the splendidly lavish Palm Court with its walls of beveled mirrors, trellises, marble pillars and its apricot and cream palette. He led me to a table to the left of the elaborately sculptured gilded central fountain—Ivana's favorite table, actually. With an effusive smile and a smooth flick of his wrist he lifted the sign that said RESERVED from the table and, pulling out an oval-backed chair, seated me in it.

Some people I knew waved and nodded and I returned the gesture. I ordered high tea. It was the least I could do after they had given me someone else's table. Tea was served in a silver teapot with a silver strainer. I poured it out and held the cup in my hands and sighed with the simple pleasure of its warmth. I took a sip and felt the scalding brew flush into my body.

I planned on staying there under the lofty ceiling listening to a quartet play until my body warmed right through. Lord Merriweather and his wife stopped by my table.

'Hello, dear. Are you here on your own?' he asked, leaning heavily on his walking stick.

'Yes. I thought I'd treat myself,' I said, looking up with a smile.

Both smiled back warmly.

'How are Wombat and Poppet?' Lady Merriweather asked.

'They're fine,' I replied.

Wombat and Poppet were my father's and Ivana's nicknames. We all had infantile nicknames in our circle. We were all Bow-wow, Cookie, Pip or Squeak or something just as babyish. The names were derived from our childhood days and carefully preserved through old age.

So my father was Wombat, because his first name was William and when he was taken as a toddler to Australia he called himself Willie Wombat. Ivana was Poppet. She was not born a lady. She met my father when she was nursing my mother and it was his nickname for her, so when he married her after my mother died, everyone was so eager to please him they quickly adopted it.

This immaturity generally served two purposes. Not having one would instantly announce you as an alien to our set. In fact, even the act of using another's first name would imply a lack of intimacy, a suggestion that you met after their childhood days were dispensed with, and were therefore not of the same class. The second and more important purpose means an outsider could never become part of the set.

'I'll give her a buzz this weekend,' Lady Merriweather said.

'She'll love that, Lilibet,' I replied. Her nickname was Lilibet because she couldn't pronounce Elizabeth when she was a child.

After they shuffled away, I ate finger sandwiches of smoked salmon, cucumber, and chicken from the silver cake stand. They were delicious. I was hungry. Really hungry. Next I tucked into a warm soft scone that I generously filled with a thick layer of silky cream and jam. A rose macaroon followed that, and finally an inch of a sinfully gooey chocolate layer cake.

When I could eat no more I was ready. I knew exactly what I wanted to do and no one was going to stop me. Least of all well-meaning, disgraced, horribly unhappy, silky-haired Dr. Kane.

17

Marlow

If you want to hit a man in the chest, aim for his groin."

—Bat Masterson

Beryl had just gone and I was sitting there staring into a glass of whiskey when the door suddenly opened. I looked up and there she was, a goddamn gorgeous goddess.

For a moment we stared at each other. Me startled and with pulses racing and her with strangely gleaming eyes.

'How did you get in?'

She shrugged. 'Beryl. I hope you don't mind. I wouldn't like to get her into trouble.'

What are you doing here? I wanted to ask but I couldn't. The whole world had faded away. There was only her, me and that office and we were hanging by a thread at the edge of the universe. I stared at her as if I was in a dream.

She moved lazily, sinuously toward me: each step like a move from the dance of the seven veils. She unbuckled the belt of her mohair coat and shrugged it off in a careless movement. It slid to the floor with a soft thud.

Underneath she was wearing a plain black shift. Her hands moved to the nape of her neck. I heard the sound of a zip grinding down. She pinched the material of her dress at her shoulders, lifted it off her body and let it fall. It puddled around her.

I inhaled sharply.

In the dim of my office, her body was so white it glowed pale against her black underwear. Everything about her warned. Expensive. Sexy. Mysterious. Forbidden. In fact, she didn't seem real. As if after I left her in the conservatory she really had turned into some sort of mythological water nymph. She slipped both her hands behind her and her bra popped open, then she allowed it to fall by the wayside. Her breasts were round and red-tipped.

The instant I saw them I wanted them in my mouth.

She hooked her fingers into her panties. Small as they were, they were the last bastion between me and all rational thought. *Don't,* I wanted to cry out, but my throat was locked tight. I *wanted* to see what the scrap of cloth covered. Her hands lingered and my eyes shifted for a second to hers. She was staring at me. And looking into her eyes was like looking into a mirror. It was brimming over with raw lust. Just a pure, unadulterated, unapologetic, unquestioning need to fuck.

This was a woman who didn't get the meaning of a cock tease. She didn't know what it was to play hard to get. Her truth filled the air and then her hands began to move down and as much as I wanted to follow them to the best kind of madness, I could not let go of her eyes. They were so precious.

I kept her eyes as she moved closer. Until I could resist the madness no more. Then I looked down. And I fucking sighed at the sight. Beautiful. My eyes caressed the blonde curls at the apex of her thighs. Totally nude she came to me and with her shoe pushed back my chair. Then she slipped between the desk and me and popped herself up on it. She put her feet on either side of me and placing her palms flat on the table behind her, she spread her knees.

Wide.

My eyes opened like those of a schoolboy in a sweetshop. I stared riveted by the way her pretty little pussy had parted open and offered all its secrets, every single whorl of pink flesh was mine to look at, drool over, and...*possess*. As I watched, thick honey collected and slowly rolled down her sex. The insides of her perfect thighs were shimmering with it.

Like a man in a trance I extended a hand and inserted my finger into her dripping hole.

With a strangled sound she threw her head back, exposing the long, white curve of her throat. My finger curled and stroked the beautifully lubricated muscles inside her. They replied by squeezing my finger helplessly. I extracted the finger. She didn't like that one bit. She whimpered restlessly and her hips slid forward slightly as if to give chase to my finger.

I bent my head and put my nose in her blonde curls, and inhaled. It sent a shock of electricity through my groin. Ah, yes. The real scent of Lady Olivia. I ran my tongue along the slit. She tasted exactly as I knew she would—like heaven. I sucked her sex and felt her flesh start swelling in my mouth. She purred with pleasure. I took my mouth away and looked at her pussy. Reddened. Glistening. Begging for it.

'I love your body,' I whispered into her soaking flesh.

'Fuck me ... Dr. Kane.'

She didn't have to ask. My cock was throbbing and standing to attention like Nelson's Column. I took my trousers off, let them drop to the floor, yanked my boxers down and stepped out of them. Then I opened a drawer and extracted a condom packet. I ripped the plastic covering open, fished one out, chucked the foil, and stretched it over my girth. I looked at her. She was staring at my dick, her mouth was trembling beautifully.

'Lie back,' I ordered.

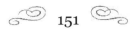

She immediately lay back on my desk, her blonde hair spreading out over the dark surface. I'd been wanting to suck her tits ever since she had dropped her bra. I leaned forward and sucked a red-tipped breast. Her flesh was soft and smooth and her nipple hard. She moaned and arched her back. Yes, exactly as I thought she would. I bit the nub in my mouth! She opened her eyes and stared at me.

'Yes, I like that,' she said in a shocked whisper.

'I know,' I muttered.

I took her nipple back into my mouth and sucked it hard and pushed two fingers into her. She writhed under me. I lifted my head, took my fingers out of her and slipped them into her mouth. She sucked them obediently. I looked down at her. Spread open on my table. All mine to do with as I pleased. And I knew exactly what I wanted to do to her. I pulled her toward me until her butt was hanging off the table. To her credit she never protested or showed any fear. She allowed me to do as I pleased.

I took hold of her ankles and crossed them while she stared at me with enormous dilated eyes. I bent her crossed ankles toward her face until her sex rose up and became a red, protruding mound of beckoning flesh between her thighs. She was incredibly flexible. I pushed her ankles so far forward I knew I must have pushed her to the very edge of discomfort, if not pain, but she bore it without complaint.

I wanted to wait. I wanted to watch her expressive, eager face a little longer. I wanted to play with the swollen flesh that poked out from between her thighs, but my cock was twitching impatiently. I had a raging need to be inside her, pounding her, watching her cry with pleasure. I wanted to claim that pussy as mine.

I wanted to obliterate all the other thoughts of the men who had used her.

Her position meant I had to force my cock into the tightly clamped walls of her sex. Her mouth opened into a shocked O. Her toes curled. And still I fed more of my length into her. The O became a sharply indrawn breath. I pushed deeper in. She winced.

But there was still more to go.

I sank another two inches and a cry came from her mouth even as she pushed herself toward me, farther impaling herself onto my rod. Why, she was insatiable! No wonder she was in my blood, beautiful, spoilt, rich, fucking Lady Olivia. At that moment she spoilt all other women for me.

There was still an inch to go, but I pulled out of her while she milked me by squeezing her muscles tightly. I hovered at the lips of her sex and then without warning I slammed into her. She cried out, her hands gripping the desk edge so hard the knuckles were bone-white.

'Is this what you wanted?' I growled.

'More,' she cried.

It was surprising that she could even take this. How on earth was she able to ask for more?

I pounded her sticky, greedy sex furiously, our pubic bones grinding until I came with a roar. It ripped through me with a shockingly violent force. At first the blood in my ears was the only thing I heard and then it was like lava pouring down a mountain, fiery, destructive, indestructible. No one and nothing could contain me.

She must have been holding onto her orgasm because she climaxed a few seconds later. I watched her mingle pleasure and pain and come with an orgasm the like of which I had never seen. Her entire body convulsed and shook so hard I had to tighten my grip on her body. When it ebbed away she was left breathing hard, her eyes glazed and shocked. I eased out of her and guided the condom off. I pulled up my boxers and my pants, zipping them as I moved slightly away. Her feet hit the carpet.

I looked out of the window. I could see us reflected in the glass. Two ghostly figures. Fuck! I had just messed up. Real bad. I heard her walk away and as much as I tried not to, I *had* to turn back to watch. There was an unsteady wobble to her legs as she walked toward her clothes. She bent to pick them up and I saw her sex, engorged and overripe. And I sensed my own restless, unsatisfied state.

My cock felt agonizingly heavy and turgid. It seemed inconceivable, but I needed to have still more, much more of her. It was impossible to know why my desire for her was so strong or so unquenchable, but there was no more denying it. That was an experiment doomed to failure even before I had conceived it. She was pulling on her panties with her back turned to me.

'Stop,' I muttered.

She turned slowly, her panties around her thighs, and looked at me.

'I'm not finished,' I said softly.

She smiled. 'Good. Because I'm thirsty.' She pulled down her panties and walked toward me. She stood in front of me and her clever hands went to work. The buttons of my trousers popped open noiselessly. Those clever hands. The zip tore down with impressive efficiency. She unbuttoned my shirt quickly and eased it over my shoulders. Her eyes moved quickly over my shoulders, chest and abs.

Then she got on her knees in front of me, looking upwards, naked, an almost penitent expression on her face. She pushed her head slightly so the head of my cock rested on her pink lower lip, the weight of it making her pout. She appeared to be waiting for me to act. Grabbing a fistful of her hair, I gently pulled her back so her throat was almost perfectly aligned, a straight passage from her mouth to her stomach. Instinctively, she opened her mouth and my cock slipped in and rested on her tongue. She had a small mouth and the bulk of it seemed to surprise her to realize that her mouth was already full. Her lips stretched.

I stroked her soft hair.

Moving my hips I began to feed my shaft slowly into her warm, silky mouth, slipping across her tongue. It was a huge turn-on to see my dick slowly disappearing into her face as she gazed up into my eyes from her position of total subjugation. It was a high, a sense of control.

As soon as I hit the soft wall at the back of her throat, I pressed into her tonsils and felt her throat contract about my head as she gagged. I pulled back, but it was only a small respite, because I went inward again, this time not content with slithering my way into the back of her mouth, but going farther to level her throat open and wedge myself into it. Again she gagged and instinctively tried to resist, but her submissive position made her attempts puny and I hardly registered them.

I pulled her head down harder, and forced my hips deeper in. Her eyes widened with surprise. And then it happened. I didn't have to train her. She was already well trained. Her throat surrendered and opened fully. My cock slid in unhindered, victorious. About an inch of me was inside that delicious tight, liquid-satin passage.

Meticulously, I fed her an inch at time, feeling the delectable squeeze of her throat. Every swallow was a silken caress, a pleasant massage. Six inches in. Seven inches. She made no sound. Her eyes were frozen wide. When she thought she was choking and her tongue writhed against me like velvet, I stopped moving, pulled her head farther down still, and waited it out. Until her throat stopped closing and relaxed again.

There was not a thing she could do to resist. To stop me. I could go as deep as I liked. Eight inches. And still I continued, an unhurried thick snake pushing into her throat until her face was pressed into my groin.

I knew with my cock so deep in her throat there was no way she could breathe so I began to pull back enjoying the way her throat squeezed to eject the foreign object out.

I kept my dick in the warm cave of her mouth while she took gasping breaths. When I judged that she had recovered I completely buried myself into her face. The slick capitulation, the depth of my penetration, and the total control I had over her served up a sensation that was like distilled pleasure. Something incandescent that pulsed down my length. I was coming and I was determined to hold as much of my cock down her throat as I could right through my climax.

As I began to shoot my load, emptying myself directly into her stomach, she began to make swallowing motions. Every spurt was a new wave of slick muscles running down my length. As the last few pulses hit my body I pulled out from her throat and filled her mouth with my remaining seed.

Before she could swallow it I used the extra lubrication of my cum to force my cock deep into her throat. Fucking her throat prolonged my ejaculation. Drops of semen and saliva escaped from around the corners of her lips and dribbled down her jaw. Her lips were slimy and her fine hair was glued to her cheek with my spill. Her breasts heaved. Tears from choking were set like jewels in her eyelashes.

She was every man's fantasy come true.

I pulled out of her mouth and watched her lick her lips. She stood up, her lower face covered with my cream, and said, 'Thanks for the drink, it was delicious, but...' She took my fingers in her small hand and guided them between her legs. 'You made my pussy wet.'

She was indeed wet. She was soaking.

I should have felt the sting of shame and guilt. How could I? I had never behaved in such an unprofessional manner before. I opened my mouth. I didn't know what I was going to say—perhaps I was intending to apologize, even knowing that an apology was only going to make it worse—but she pressed my lips with her index finger.

'Shh... Say nothing,' she said, shaking her head slowly. '*Nothing* has changed. I'll see you Wednesday at the agreed time.'

Then she was gone.

Ah, but, Lady Olivia, *everything* has changed.

18

Olivia

The earth laughs in flowers.
—Ralph Waldo Emerson

After I left Dr. Kane I found it impossible to stay in London. All I wanted to do was go to his flat and let him fuck me, but I was afraid he would start to imagine that I was some kind of stalker. So when Ivana told me that she was sending around the car to take me back to Marlborough Hall in time for dinner I readily agreed.

I had ten minutes before I had to go and get dressed for dinner so I went into the conservatory and checked on the plastic pots where my flower seeds were germinating. I was putting on my gardening gloves when Ivana walked in.

'Hello, darling. I wasn't here when you came in.' She kissed me warmly on my cheeks. 'How are you?' Her gaze was searching.

'All right,' I said quietly.

'I've been meaning to ask you, how are your sessions with Dr. Kane coming on?'

I felt suddenly guarded. I could not let anyone know what had happened between Dr. Kane and me. It was my fault any way. I had practically forced him. I took my gloves off, looked up at her and smiled. 'Good.'

She smiled brightly. 'Does that mean you are starting to remember things?'

'A bit.'

Her smile faltered. 'What does that mean?'

'It just means that Dr Kane doesn't want to push it.'

A slight frown was trying to form on her smooth forehead, but the Botox injections held firm. 'What have you actually remembered?'

'A few things. Nothing truly important. A birthday party. Walking up to the bell tower. Going to dance school.'

She was staring at me with an unimpressed expression.

'They are little things,' I said. 'I know they sound unimportant to you because you have all your memories, but they are very important to me because I have nothing.'

'I see,' she said carefully.

'The main thing is I feel really well.'

Her eyes narrowed. 'He hasn't acted...in any way irresponsibly, has he?'

I could feel my cheeks becoming hot but I made my eyes large as if shocked. 'Of course not.'

'I hope not. Because I would be absolutely furious if he tried anything with you. I overlooked his past and gave him the benefit of the doubt, even though I was advised not to use him, because I trusted him.'

'Ivana, I'm a grown woman. You don't have to protect me as if I was a child.'

She looked slightly hurt. 'You're right, of course. I'm sorry. I don't mean to stifle you. I just can't help it. You've always been so delicate. I've always felt responsible.'

I reached out and touched her hand. 'Thank you. I know you want the best for me, but please don't worry. Dr. Kane is a good man.'

She smiled suddenly, a bright Ivana smile. This one could melt icebergs. 'On another topic, Wills is coming for dinner tonight.'

I cringed inwardly. No wonder she wanted me back. Wills, or William Henry Asquith the seventh, was the dullard son of a penniless duke who lived three miles away. It was always hoped that we would marry. He had the better title and I the money. To be perfectly honest I suspected he was a closet homosexual, but I knew she had gone to a lot of trouble to set up the dinner and I really didn't want to upset her. Besides, my sister had said she would be there and I could always count on her to take the edge off a boring night.

'That's nice,' I said politely.

'Why don't you wear your blue dress? The one with the sweetheart neckline that we got from Browns. It makes you look quite simply stunning.'

'That's a good idea. I will do that.'

She smiled with satisfaction. 'Right. I had better crack on. It's been a bit of a nightmare day and there's so much to do. One of the horses foaled last night. Have to go and check how mother and son are doing. See you later?'

'OK.'

She turned away and began to walk out.

'Ivana?' I called.

She turned around. 'Yes, darling?'

'Thank you for everything you've done for me. I do really appreciate it.'

Her face misted over. 'I'd love to do more. You are my daughter. Not of flesh, but of spirit.'

We smiled at each other and then she was gone.

Dinner was a dreary affair. It turned out that Daffy decided not to come after all. She went to a party in Fulham instead. Of course Ivana was a wonderful hostess, but Daddy couldn't stop talking about the new foal. And Wills kept giving me puppy dog looks, which were irritating at best. It was even possible that he was plucking up the courage to ask me out. I invented a headache and excused myself early.

'Do you want me to send Bertie up with some hot chocolate for you,' Ivana asked, her face concerned.

'No,' I said, feeling really guilty. 'Please don't worry. It's nothing. I'll be fine once I take a couple of tablets.'

'Goodnight, darling,' she said with such feeling that I almost wanted to blurt the truth out to her. I was fucking Dr. Kane and I was missing him so much I couldn't even bear to sit beside Wills and put up with his fumbling attempts to court me when I knew all he really wanted to do was crawl into bed with a man.

But I didn't. I knew she wouldn't understand. Ivana and all the people in my circle placed position and status above silly little things like love and emotions.

'Goodnight.'

I went to my room and I lay down in the dark. For hours I tossed and turned and in the end I knew I had to go and see Dr. Kane. I got out of bed, dressed, left Marlborough Hall and nervously drove down to London. I hardly ever drove since my accident.

I rang on Dr. Kane's bell at two in the morning.

Marlow

I was lying on the sofa, music muted right down, and dreaming of Olivia when the doorbell went. For a second my brain went blank. I glanced at my watch. Who the fuck was ringing my bell at two in the morning? Kids? A drunk at the wrong address? It rang again. I didn't even think I expected anyone to reply when I said, 'Yeah?'

'Dr. Kane,' she said and I froze. For a few seconds there was silence and then her voice said again, 'Dr. Kane?'

I came to like a sleepwalker waking up. 'Yeah, come up,' I said.

I stood at the closed door and listened to the sound of her heels on the stairs. Then I opened the door. She stood at the second step of the stairs and looked at me with those huge eyes.

'Come on in then,' I said softly and she walked up to me. I stood aside to allow her to pass through. She had changed her perfume. It was subtle, expensive, mysterious. Exactly what I would have chosen for her. I closed the door, caught her by the arm, whirled her around and set her against the door. She looked up at me with wide eyes.

'What are you doing here?'

Her seductive mouth moved. I could feel my blood heating up. My cock stirring, hardening. I stared at her, mesmerized.

'I couldn't sleep,' she said.

We stared at each other. I couldn't sleep either.

'I can't,' I said, my eyes moving from her mouth to her eyes and back to her mouth. Her chest was heaving. 'Fucking resist you,' I said, and grabbing both her hands, pinned them over her head.

She opened that plump mouth to say something and I crushed it with mine. She made a strangled sound. I slipped my tongue into her mouth. My free hand found the buckle and the zip at the back of her skirt. I slid my hand across the crotch of her panties.

'You're so fucking wet.'

I pushed the material to one side and plunged a finger deep into her pussy.

She moaned and arched her body so her breasts pressed into my chest.

I rammed two fingers in. 'Is this what you came here for?'

She closed her eyes and shuddered. 'Yes.'

I took off her top. The little half-cup bra I just pushed down. I bent my head and bit the rosy nipple.

'Dr. Kane,' she whimpered.

'My name is Marlow.'

Her eyes fluttered open. They were dilated and smoky with desire.

I added a third finger into the mix.

She leaned her head back against the door and moaned. I pulled my fingers out and slid my track bottoms down my hips. My cock sprang out hard and ready. I lifted her right leg and draped it around my hips so her sex opened up all swollen and wet and hungry. Her clit was engorged and extended. I pinched the hood, pulled it back and exposed her center, small, white, über sensitive and mine. I wanted to suck it. But not yet. Now I was too riled. Too desperate to be inside her.

I grabbed her right thigh and held it so she could not move and I impaled myself on her. It was urgent and merciless and without warning. She screamed. I didn't stop. I continued to push myself into her until I was balls deep.

I fucked her so hard her body jerked like a puppet. Watching her utterly powerless as she writhed and groaned and slapped into my body was addictive. I loved to see her in that position. Totally open to me. Vulnerable. Totally dominated. I felt Herculean.

'Oh fuck,' I growled.

I could feel my orgasm coming so I reluctantly pulled out of her and jerked off all over her blonde curls. Still panting I looked at my handiwork. Like water droplets caught on a spider's web the milky white drops were all over her. With my hand I streaked it into her skin and gathering some in my fingers held it a few inches from her mouth.

We stared at each other. Her lips were trembling. She leaned forward and I pulled my fingers back and she leaned farther forward and caught my fingers in her mouth. We stared at each other as she sucked my fingers clean.

'My turn,' I said and got down on my knees. I threw her thigh over my shoulder and, burying my face in her pussy, slid my tongue into her and lapped at the dripping walls. She grabbed my shoulders and thrust forward desperately. I moved my head back.

'That's right, babe. Ride me,' I encouraged lustily before plunging my tongue back into her throbbing sex. While I fucking devoured her flesh she rocked her hips on my mouth and teeth until she came with a piercing shriek and a rush of goose bumps.

Olivia

We went into his bedroom. More like a monk's cell. Bare walls, a plain double bed, cheap scratchy sheets, a cupboard and two side tables. He sheathed that incredible cock of his and took me while I was on my hands and knees. It was wild and violent and magnificently beautiful. I tried to catch my breath, but our climax sucked us into a vortex of ecstasy. I shuddered uncontrollably. And when it died away my breath was ragged. I fought back sweet tears, but they would not be checked. The carnal smell of our coupling enveloped us like a fog. He touched a tear glimmering on my lashes wonderingly.

'You're so beautiful.'

I couldn't tell him I was sorry he had not deposited his seed in my womb. That it had not coated my insides and grown into something.

I realized it then. He was my journey home.

He pulled out of me. 'We have to talk,' he said.

'No, we don't. Let it be just sex for a while. I know it will all probably unravel when you tell me whatever it is you are hiding from me, but for now I'm happy with this. I am asking for nothing more than what I have now.'

'Oh, Olivia. What a mess I have made of this whole thing.'

'It's not your fault. I forced myself on you. And I don't regret it. Whatever happens I will never regret this.'

He took off his shirt and I saw what I had not noticed the other evening at the office. Located on his fabulously muscular pecs, just over his heart, were two white ink tattoos in the shape of teardrops. They were not beautiful. Not in the least. They reminded me of scars, raised, white and born of pain. I reached out a hand and touched one of them. He flinched, then became still. I looked up at him, my hand hovering in the air. His eyes were deliberately blank.

'Who are they?' I asked, but even as the words formed in my throat I already knew.

'My children.' He looked down at the tattoos. 'That's Roxy and that's Rick.'

'I'm sorry. I'm so sorry about them.'

'Yes, so am I.' All the light leached out of his eyes.

'They were very young, weren't they?'

'Yes, Roxy was five and Rick was four.' And he looked so bleak and wretched I wanted to hold him tight.

'Oh, Marlow.'

He shook his head. 'It's OK,' he said. 'It was another lifetime. I've learned to live with it now. I'm all right.' And then he sank onto the bed and, running his hand through his hair, sighed sadly. 'It's OK,' he said again, as if he was not talking to me but comforting himself even though he knew it could never be repaired.

'Will you tell me about them?' I asked.

He looked up at me, his beautiful, kind eyes pained. 'I can't. I just can't. Not yet.'

19

Marlow

We depart with a thousand regrets in our hearts.
—Omar Khayyam

After Olivia left the next morning I went into the top shelf of my cupboard and brought out the envelope that was there. It was only two years old but it was gray with use. I had read it so many times I almost knew it by heart. Each word burned into my mind and still smoking after all this time. There were four pages to the letter. I opened them. The creases were so ingrained, they were soft and powdery, the ink gone from them.

I stared at the first page.

Her writing: neat, controlled, small and familiar. So familiar. Oh! Maria. I remember she used to write me love notes and put them into the lunchboxes she insisted on making for me. They wouldn't say much...

I'm wearing no panties. When you come home, come find me, and without saying a word fuck me. xMina

Or it would say...

When you eat these corned beef sandwiches, just remember I thought of you while I was spreading the mustard and I will think of you all day until you return to me and spread my legs. xMina

But she had not left her last letter to be found by me. She had posted it. It arrived a day after the 'incident'. At that time I was so shocked I read the whole thing twice and could not understand anything.

For days afterwards I had stared at it without any real comprehension. I mean, I understood the meaning of every word and I got each sentence when taken separately, but as a whole, in context: what the fuck was it all about? What the hell was she going on about?

Then I would think of her buying that grenade. I mean, who does that? Who blows themselves up with a grenade? People gas themselves in the privacy of their garage or take sleeping pills or slit their wrists, and the really scary ones launch themselves off buildings, but grenades? Wow! And afterwards, buying all those gas canisters just to make sure that nothing worth saving would come out of her bonfire.

If total annihilation with an audience was her intention she certainly succeeded. I saw it all happen in slow motion: the explosion, red first, then blossoming into orange, the middle turning white, then back to orange and red. Then smoke: thick, black, acrid smoke. I had lain on the ground and watched the car's doors fly away, the glass shattering outwards and upwards, while all around me fiery debris rained from the sky. Roxy's shoe was the hard part. The way it landed next to me, charred and heartbreakingly small.

Like a taunt. See, how powerful I am.

I used to stare into the bottom of a glass of whiskey and replay the memory of her, as she was the day before she died, chewing on an apple, laughing, an almost sublime expression on her face, as she watched me playing with the children. How could a woman wearing such an expression be thinking of ending it all the next day?

There had been nothing. Nothing to tell me she was unhappy, upset, or standing on the verge of committing suicide and taking our children with her. It was the most perplexing, shocking thing. Finally, I phoned her best friend.

'Did you know that Maria thought we were having an affair?'

'What?' she had almost shouted down the phone.

'She thought we were having an affair,' I repeated.

'Where did she get that idea from?'

'I don't know.'

'Then why would *you* think that?'

'She left a letter.'

'A letter? Accusing us of having an affair? I can't believe it. I'd like to see that letter.'

'No,' I refused. I didn't want her to know that Maria had referred to her as that two-faced, long-titted, no nipple, skinny-assed, cock-sucking, cum bucket.

She went silent.

'Did she seem colder toward you or change in any way?' I insisted.

'No. We were best friends. We told each other everything,' she denied, suspicion creeping into her voice. She was beginning to doubt the existence of the letter. She was like all human beings—she would rather believe a lie than accept that she had been so thoroughly fooled.

We ended the conversation on an uneasy note.

I called her other close friends. Did she say anything to you? The answer was always the same. No. No. No. No. I phoned her brother. He put the phone down on me in disgust.

Often I dreamed of my children. We were in a garden or a schoolroom. There were other children playing there with them. I called to them and they came running to me. I picked them up and held them tightly, relief pouring through my veins.

'Thank God! Thank God. It was just a nightmare. I dreamed you were both dead.'

'Like Grandma and Grandad?' they asked me.

'Like Grandma and Granddad,' I told them, laughing and crying at the same.

'But we are not real, Daddy,' they told me solemnly. And then I woke up with tears pouring down my face. Wishing I had not woken up. Convinced they were still alive in another dimension.

Weeks later after the furore had died down, and after the hospital foundation had used words like 'regretfully', 'untenable' and 'tarnished reputation', the great thaw arrived. And with it came rage. How I cursed her. Bitch. Fucking stupid cunt.

It was so bad all my breaths become gasps of anger. I had to stop seeing friends. I was seriously at risk of totally, completely, unequivocally and corrosively losing my shit if another one said, 'God wanted his little angels back so he called them home,' or some other similar crap.

I wanted to spit at them. 'Oh right! Is that why he chose to burn them to death? God didn't do this, you fucking moron!'

During that period I opened the letter often and ended up slamming my fist on my desk so hard I eventually broke the damn thing. I was so furious once I decided to burn her letter in the fireplace, but my hand shook as I tried to throw it in: I couldn't destroy something I hadn't yet understood.

Months later I was carefully unfolding her letter and finally trying to understand my part in it. I no longer raged against her or her abusers who had turned her into a monster. The season of guilt had come. It was worse than the rage. Far worse. Oh the guilt. How it ate at my insides! It was all my fault for being so blind and so caught up with my own success that I never saw it. Not once.

Ever seen the way a team of termites can utterly decimate a tree until it is nothing but a shell?

That was what my guilt did to me. I walked around, an empty shell. I walked, I talked, I ate, I worked, but inside I was dead. There was no way to atone for what I had done. She was gone and she had taken my innocent children with her.

Olivia was gone, but her scent still lingered on my skin. I held the letter in my hand and it felt lighter somehow. Because for the first time I understood.

I held up a page:

When I am gone I will watch you and I will remember us. Our bodies spilled together. The light slanting into the room. The coffee cups with dregs. The croissant crumbs on the plate. One plate. We shared it remember?

Your breath on my skin. Your hand on my breast. Your leg thrown over mine. Your flesh. My flesh. Joined. Stuck. Forever. Forever.

Do you hear me, Dr. big shot Marlow Kane?

Forever. No matter who you touch. Who you fuck with that great, big, dirty cock of yours.

I know what big daddy long dick likes. I know all your secrets.

You think I don't know how many cunts you have entered. Do they feel as silky as mine? Do they call your name when you are fucking them in the ass?

You like that, don't you?

You start at the mouth, after a little while you move to the cunt, then when that insatiable cock of yours is nicely coated with pussy slime, you plunder the ass. And then you bring that shitty cock home and put it in my mouth.

You asshole, you! I'm still dripping with your fucking semen.

There was much more, four pages of the same insanely jealous, crude, totally baseless ranting—I was always faithful to her—but I won't go on. You get the picture. I was a careless, blind fool who never understood that she had loved me with an intensity I did not feel or even guess at. I had loved her, but not the way she had loved me.

177

Wood only understands what it is to burn when it meets a flame. Olivia was my flame. She made me burn. She made me understand what poor, damaged Maria had felt: that all-consuming passion to possess someone so completely that renders death preferable to not having it. I never had the ability to miss anyone. Until now. Now I missed her the moment she left my presence.

With sadness I remembered the times Maria had said, 'Come back to bed.' And I had kissed her lightly on her forehead and hurried away to immerse myself in my work. She had rightly construed that as a lack of emotion. If Olivia asked me to come back to bed under no circumstances would I be heading off in the opposite direction.

For so long I had kept her poisonous letter. As if I deserved to suffer. Deserved to read her crazy lies. Now, I went to the fireplace, turned the gas on, and watched the flames rise up. I dropped the letter into them and watched the orange flames lick around the edges of the papers. Browning, curling, and finally consuming them until they were blackened ashes that fell into the grate. It was poetic.

The cremation of Maria's letter.

As I watched the ashes began to fly into the room and for the first time there was no guilt or rage, only a lingering sense of profound loss for my children and for their loss: they would never experience kindergarten, get high behind a bicycle shed, fall in love, get married or know the great joy of having children of their own.

'Time is the greatest healer. It will be less painful,' everybody said, but time had made no difference. At night I still saw the flames reflected in their eyes as I ran in slow motion toward them.

I hurt as much today as I ever did and I guess I always will.

20

Olivia

Though we had sex, twice, before I left Dr. Kane's home that morning I longed for him all day, and even knowing I had an appointment with him the next day I found it impossible to wait another night, another morning and another afternoon before I saw him again. So I phoned Beryl and she told me his last appointment should leave about five thirty so if I would come around about that time she'd slip me in.

I spent a long time getting ready. I wore my new perfume and because I knew Marlow liked playing with my hair, stroking it, twisting it in his fist, I washed it and brushed it until it shone. Then I pushed a blue velvet Alice band on my head to keep it away from my face.

I put on a red dress that I had bought that afternoon. It was not something I would normally have considered. It was a bit fast with a zip that went from its plunging neckline all the way down to its immodest hemline. I slipped on a pair of high heels exactly the same color as my Alice band, also acquired that day, and I was ready for Marlow Kane's pleasure.

Underneath the cheap red dress I was nude.

When I arrived, Beryl whistled at me and made me blush. We chatted for a bit before she packed up her bag to leave. After I heard Beryl close the door, I took off my coat and I opened his office door. I closed it behind me and posed against it. I had interrupted him in some deep thought because it took a moment for his eyes to stir and quicken with desire.

I unzipped the fast dress all the way down. His eyes never left me. I let it fall to the ground and walked slowly, my hips swaying exaggeratedly, over to his window. I kicked my shoes off and leaning forward laid my palms on the windowsill. I could see the street below. There were people and any one of them could have looked up and seen me naked. I didn't care. With my legs spread wide I pushed my naked bottom out invitingly, and turned my head to the side to look at him.

He was only a few steps away, his face full of pure lust. He stood and came forward and bent his head toward me. I felt his breath, hot and urgent, hit the side of my neck, and then his fist was twisting in my hair...and tugging. My head jerked back. I stared up at him. His face was dark and his eyes blazed with need. A

hand was caressing the curve of my bottom.
He slapped it.

'What is it you want, Lady Olivia?' he asked
quietly.

I felt excitement like a tingle on my skin.
Staring into his eyes I formed my words. 'I
want your big cock in my ass, Dr. Kane.'

Marlow

My reaction was to become so completely
still that it was the opposite of a reaction.

Her face paled, then reddened with shame.
Her pliant body stiffened. 'Sorry. Have I
overstepped the mark? Was that too
disgusting?' Her voice faltered. :oor thing, she
tried to laugh it off, but she was humiliated.

My hand was still twisted in her hair.
Maria's words were ashes in my mouth. There
she was again taunting me. *You start at the
mouth, after a little while you move to the
cunt, then when that insatiable cock of yours
is nicely coated with pussy slime, you
plunder the ass. And then you bring that
shitty cock home and put it in my mouth. You
asshole, you! I'm still dripping with your
fucking semen.*

But it was completely untrue. I didn't do
that to her. To start with I was never
unfaithful to her. Not even straight sex, let

alone anal sex. And I was not crazy mad for anal sex either.

Twice in four years we had anal sex. Both times she initiated it. I guess I just didn't particularly want anal sex with her. I looked down at Olivia, her poor crumpled face and her innocent offer in tatters all around her.

And I smiled. A slow smile. *The difference is, Maria, I didn't want your ass, but I, oh God, how I want to be in Olivia's.*

I wanted it so bad Maria's taunt was almost true. Never again was I going to allow her to ruin the special thing I had with Olivia.

Here's the reply to your repulsive letter, Maria.

Fuck you! How dare you blame me, you selfish, psychopathic murderer, you? You killed *my* kids. I never deliberately tried to harm you, and it's not my fault that I didn't love you the way you loved me. That's just life. Tough. Get over it.

And guess what else? When I finish fucking Olivia's ass I plan to hold open her ass cheeks and watch my semen drip out of it. And you know what else? Maybe I'll even lick it all up. Because I'm *dirty*. Far, far more than you could ever have imagined.

Olivia

'Without lube?' His voice was a growl.

For a second there I was terrified that he was angry or disgusted. He was definitely shocked, but then the desire came back into his eyes, burning stronger than before, and I pushed my bottom against his hardness and said, 'I'm lubed and ready.'

'Well, then. On your toes.'

I obeyed instantly. His hands grabbed my hips and roughly slanted them upwards so my sex was tilted right up and screaming 'mind the gap'. He got to his knees and, holding my butt cheeks apart, buried his face in my exposed sex. I felt his nose part my folds as his tongue ravished my clit. The position was dirty and sexy and blood rushed up to my head. 'Ah,' I groaned as a thick finger dipped into my slick wetness and immediately found its way inside my ass. Slowly it rotated, stretching and preparing me.

'Rock your hips,' he ordered and I could feel his breath hitting my clit.

I rode his jutting tongue. The double sensation was incredible, almost...hypnotic.

'Faster,' he commanded.

I obeyed instantly, rocking and frantically fucking his mouth and tongue until every cell in my body melted like butter in a hot oven and I was no longer the strange girl without any memory, but a liquid pool of indescribable pleasurable. I had never felt so fulfilled. So utterly satisfied. I had hardly returned to the state of being Olivia again when he moved away from my body.

'Wait here,' he instructed and moved away from my body. I saw him pick up a cushion from the long sofa at the other end of the room and come back with it. He held it in front of me and with a hand on the small of my back he guided me forward until the pillow was wedged between my groin and the windowsill. I heard his trousers fall to the ground and felt his hard cock push into my slick sex.

'Oh, Doctor,' I breathed, shuddering with pleasure and pushing myself onto the deliciously thick shaft. Leisurely, with total control, and without any urgency, he fucked me a few times, then withdrew and rubbed the bulbous head of his cock, now thickly varnished with pussy honey, over the puckered entrance of my butt.

'This is my beautiful ass,' he said. 'I fucking own it. I don't need permission from you or anyone else to fill it. I'll slide in whenever I feel like it and stay for as long as I want. Do you understand?'

'Yes,' I groaned. 'Oh God, yes.' I *ached* to be filled by him.

Behind me I felt his body shake with hunger. I didn't need to be told. I relaxed my body and waited while he very slowly, inch by inch, stopping every now and again to acclimatize me to the intrusion, forced himself into me, invading and stretching the tight passage where a man should *not* be, until he was so deep in my bowels I could no longer think.

When he finally became still I exhaled with relief. He used that opportunity to push himself even deeper into my body. The muscles in my legs quivered and strained. Having him so deep in me was strange but terribly exciting. I could feel him pulsing and throbbing inside me.

I turned around and looked at him.

His eyes were hooded and dark and his jaw was clenched tight with pure lust.

'You're so fucking huge,' I whimpered.

His answer was to pull back and slam back inside.

I cried out with the electric sensation of pain, but the first flush was almost instantly replaced by wanton pleasure as he continued to slowly pump in and out of me. I found myself melting around him. I could no longer see our reflection in the windowpane. It was white with the heat of my pants. There was so much sensation coming from his cock that I felt almost dizzy. The only thing that mattered was this. Me giving him pleasure.

I clenched the shaft of meat inside me hard, as hard as I could, and he growled. It felt good to know I could do that to him. It made me feel powerful. He increased his pace. The movement was making my clit grind against the little cushion he had wedged between the edge of wood and me.

His thrusts grew more frantic and my blood-engorged clit rubbed more and more relentlessly against the cushion. I was going to climax again. My body began to tighten. As if his cock understood my body, it swelled inside me. But I could not concentrate on it anymore—the sensations that had started at my core were tearing through me like a hurricane.

I swirled out with it into a whirlpool of pure wonder. Juices gushed out of me and trickled down my thighs. I cried out over and over as he lunged into me until he erupted inside me.

Shattered, as if I had been dropped from a high place, I held onto him with my muscles and listened to the sensations inside my body. They were all subtle. They didn't want him to leave.

Slowly he pulled out.

I sighed.

He bent down and licked my sticky thighs. That was just the beginning of what he licked that night.

—Don't get too close
It's dark inside
It's where my demons hide—

21

Marlow

She lay peacefully in a deep trance in my zero gravity chair. I looked at her face, innocent and utterly trusting, and felt a fierce instinct to protect her flash through me. I had experienced it before, but never for a woman.

The first time was when my son was born and the nurse had given him to me wrapped in a blanket, a wrinkled, mottled, red and, quite frankly, ugly little thing—more changeling than human. His eyes and fists were tightly closed, and the first sensation that flooded into me was not one of joy or happiness, but stark fear.

Would I be able to protect him from this cruel world long enough for him to be able to take care of himself? The feeling had gone as quickly as it had come but I had never forgotten it. The crippling panic. It was back now. The terror of not being able to protect her until she was strong enough to protect herself. I stilled it. I knew I could get to the bottom of this mystery. I knew it was not by accident that Ivana had chosen me.

My intention that day was to return her to the day her mother died, but I wanted to take her to a safe memory first. Something she could come out with and point to as another successful session in remembering the past.

'You are safe from all harm, Olivia,' I said quietly. 'There is nothing that can harm you. You are six years old today and it is bedtime. Where are you?'

'In the tower,' she murmured. 'I've had a lovely day. There are presents all over the floor. Ivana says I can have them strewn about today but tomorrow they will all have to be put away neatly.'

'Is she there now?'

'Yes.' She smiled, child-like.

'What is she doing?'

'Ivana is reading me a story. "Why is Cinderella's stepmother so cruel?" I ask her. "Stepmothers are often portrayed like that in fairy tales," she says.

'"Why?"

'"Because they can't help being jealous of their stepdaughters, I suppose." I frown. "But you're not like that?" "No, I'm not," she says, and breaks into a cheeky grin. "But I would be if I didn't love you so much." I nod. It seems to make perfect sense to me. "Ivana?"

'"Yes, darling."

"Why didn't Cinderella tell her daddy about what her stepmother and sisters were doing to her?"

"'Perhaps because Cinderella was too nice to tell tales on anyone. And, I think, she might have thought that if her daddy knew it would have been really, really hard for him to choose between her and her stepmother since he loved them both." I frown and think about what she has said. It is quite a shocking piece of information that Cinderella's stepfather might have loved both equally. "Do you think he might have chosen the evil stepmother over good, kind Cinderella?" I ask. Ivana hides a smile. Adults are always doing that. "Probably not," she says and closes the book.

'I snuggle back into the pillows. "If I were him I'd choose Cinderella," I say. "So would I," she whispers and, kissing me goodnight, switches on the blue nightlight, and quietly leaves the room. I hear the echo of her shoes going down the steps of the tower. And then I look out into the night sky full of stars and wonder where my mother is. I start to feel more and more sleepy. I fall asleep.'

She paused and I was just about to guide her out of that memory and back to the day her mother died when she spoke again, and I realized there was more to that memory, by far more.

'The sound of scratching wakes me up. I am sleepy. I don't want to wake up, but the sound becomes louder. I open my eyes and listen... And suddenly I am awake. It is not a scratching sound that I have heard but a clicking, the clicking of a dog's nails on the stone steps coming up the tower. There is another tread coming up together with the dog. It is much heavier. And it is steady. Step by step they are coming up. I clutch my bedclothes to my chin and hold my breath. The door opens.'

Her limbs began to twitch restlessly.

'Who has come into your room?'

'Tom the gardener and his pitbull, Tiger,' she said. There is a tremor in her voice. 'I am afraid of them. I want them to go away.'

'Nothing can harm you, Olivia. You are just watching a scene from a very safe place.'

'Tiger comes into the room, his tags rattling. The sound makes me feel cold all over. He has powerful jaws and a big chest, but he is also very strong. I have seen him train with Tom in the garden. Under his shiny black fur his muscles are thick and rippling. His broad, square head turns in my direction and his small, piggy eyes find me. I am scared of Tiger.

'"Attention," Tom says, and Tiger walks into the middle of the room. From this position he will not move until Tom gives him the command to leave. His yellow eyes never blink. He opens his mouth and starts breathing noisily. Drool starts sliding from his teeth down to the floor.

"'I don't want to," I tell Tom. "Please. It's still my birthday and Daddy says I'm allowed to do anything I want on my birthday." Tom laughs. "I've got a birthday treat for you."

"'I don't want it," I say. Tiger begins to growl. The sound terrifies me. I start to cry. "Stop it," Tom scolds. "I can't bear it when you do that."

'Tiger's growl becomes more ferocious. He starts frothing. Tom makes me take my knickers off. Then he puts his mouth between my legs... And he licks and sucks me...down there... And then my head goes funny, and after a while my body starts floating.'

I sprang out of my seat, stunned, and paced the floor with my right hand pressed against my forehead. I couldn't believe it. I had found the white owl. And it was the fucking gardener! A hiss of pure hate tore from my throat. Disgust, like fingers, was in my guts, stabbing, clawing ripping. Pedophilia never ceased to amaze me, no matter how many times I heard about it. How could human beings take their sickness out on innocent little children?

The bastard. The sick, sick bastard.

My eyes filled with tears of rage. If he had been there I would have killed him with my bare hands, I swear it. I started to retch, but it was dry—the grotesque thing would not come up. I covered my face with my hands and dragged my fingers up and through my hair. I could not let her go on. I could not hear another word. I was so violently angry my body was trembling uncontrollably.

'Stop,' I screeched.

The sound was so loud in the completely silent room her body jerked. I turned and stared at her with narrowed eyes. Her eyelids fluttered and then she went still. Fuck! That was stupid. I could have shocked her out of her hypnotic state and made it all so much worse.

I felt desperate to leave the room and glug down half a bottle of JD. All I wanted to do was get rid of the filthy, ugly image that was clinging like a rotten fungus to my brain. I just didn't want to deal with it. I felt incapable of it. First Maria. Now her.

I took a deep breath and forced myself to calm down.

Now I understood why she had answered 'growl' when I had said 'dog' during the word association play. And it explained why she had allowed herself to be debased by the Invisible Society. A society that she spoke of with disgust.

It was a direct result of what that worm had done to her. By forcing her to climax in the presence of a growling dog he had rewired her child brain to connect sex with fearful circumstances. As an adult she needed danger to get the same high. So she had taken risks with her sex life. Putting her life in danger to get back the sexual high that had been forced upon her as an innocent child.

I went and stood over Olivia and gazed down at her. She was lying with her eyes closed, her face blank of all expression. Completely oblivious to what was happening around her.

My chest rose and fell with every breath I took. I experienced a strong desire to rest my cheek on top of her golden head. I was still staring at her with a mixture of longing and pity when it hit me. I had been so shocked and horrified by what the gardener had done I had missed it. Completely. I turned toward her.

'Where is the white owl, Olivia?'

And she began to shiver with absolute terror. And I knew then that whoever the white owl was, he or she was not the gardener. The little girl's fear was such that once again she was in danger of being ripped out of her trance.

'That's all right, Olivia. You've done well. You can go to your safe place now. I want you to remember a happy memory. Can you do that?'

'Yes,' she whispered, warmth flowing back into her voice, and recalled a picnic with her mother.

I brought her out with the instruction to forget everything except the picnic.

She turned and smiled at me. 'I feel really good.'

Suddenly I felt so depressed that I could barely move. All over the world other children were being abused and irreparably damaged. 'That's great,' I said and left the room.

She came out slowly. 'Is everything all right? Did something happen?'

I turned away from the window and smiled. 'Everything is just fine.'

She walked toward the couch and sat on it.

I didn't plan it. I had not even thought of it. One moment she was sitting on my couch and the next she had lifted her skirt, showed me her bare blonde pussy and said, 'Fuck me if you dare.'

And before I knew it I had stridden over to her. I was sitting on the edge of the sofa pulling my dick out of my underpants while she was upside down. Her cheek was resting on my floor close to my shoe, her elbows were bent, her palms were flat on the floor, and her legs were splayed open like a pair of scissors. I held onto her hips and plunged into her like a mad bull. The thrusts into her slender body were fierce, relentless and full of tension. Perhaps I was exorcising my demons, but her tight inner muscles recognized nothing but pleasure. They began to spasm and cramp violently as her body contorted with her orgasm. I didn't wait a second longer.

With a grunt I let myself explode inside her.

I pulled her up and rested her so she was lying face down across my thighs, and slumped back, exhausted. I closed my eyes, my hand absently stroking the smooth curve of her buttocks as both our pulses and breathing returned to normal.

'I'm hungry. Aren't you ever going to feed me anything but cock and semen?' she teased.

I couldn't show her how disturbed I was. I had to be normal. I opened my eyes and smiled down at her. 'What would you like to eat?'

'I'd like to go out to a place where they serve cocktails in jam jars. Do you know such a place?'

'I do indeed.' And I couldn't resist slipping a finger into her lovely pussy.

She giggled.

My finger was still inside her when we were interrupted by the sound of her phone ringing. She jumped guiltily. 'That will be Ivana. I had better not take it, I don't want to lie to her about where I am or who I am with.' She bit her lip. 'She doesn't know about us.'

My gut constricted! I pulled my finger out of her and she sat up and pulled her skirt down over her hips. My first instinct was to shout, *Don't tell her, don't tell anyone yet. There's so much still behind the veil.*

My horror must have shown on my face.

'Don't worry,' she said with a small smile. 'I'm not going to tell anyone. I know what they would do. They would disapprove and try to stop me from seeing you.'

I felt relief pour into my gut. Like a condemned man who is given one more day. I knew the reprieve would be short-lived and I had to get to the bottom of the white owl before anyone found out about us. We were not being discreet. Something told me I had very little time left.

I took her to Carambas and like a lovesick fool watched her eat and drink many margaritas. I knew other men were looking at her with desire. She was the cool ice-queen. So unknowable. So mysterious.

My hands went around her waist, possessively, pulling her to me. She was mine. She laughed and pulled me to the small dance floor where we bumped hips and pretended to do the samba and the merengue and the rumba. She was light and it was easy to carry her really high and swing her around my waist or pass her between my legs. She seemed so happy creating hard-on's that she would have to pay for later. I looked into her flushed face and her shining eyes were silvery and I wished it could always be like that.

She smoothed the fabric of her skirt and I remembered the first time she did that. When Beryl had engineered us into having tea in my office. Then I had watched her hands, white and fragile, and struggled with the intense desire to cover them with my own, to protect her from all the demons of her past. Now I reached forward and placed my hands over hers. They were so small they disappeared completely underneath mine.

She looked up surprised. 'What?' she asked.

I shook my head. 'Nothing. Nothing at all.'

A young girl, possibly still in her teens came up to our table. She was pretty much wasted. 'You're Lady O, aren't you?' she shouted above the music.

I felt a tremor of fear run through Olivia. She turned to me like a child. I smiled reassuringly as if I were her parent.

She turned to the girl. 'Yes, I guess I am,' she said.

The girl said. 'I'm so glad you're OK. After the accident, I mean.'

'Thank you.'

'Oh and I really liked that green dress you wore to the Ascot races last year.'

'Thank you.'

'Ok then byeeeee,' the girl called as she was pulled away to the dance floor by one of her friends.

Olivia turned to me.

'You did brilliant,' I encouraged.

She smiled.

And WHOA sunlight suddenly burst into my heart. I was shocked by the intensity and force of the sensation and I think I made up my mind then. I was going to destroy all the records. I was never going to tell her about the abuse or the Invisible Society. Her brain had hidden it away for a reason. She was happy. She was no longer that person. Why bring it back? I helped Maria to remember and where did it get her? In the middle of a bonfire, that's where.

Perhaps it was better to let sleeping dogs lie.

Let the white owl remain in the past. Perhaps the white owl didn't even exist anymore. Perhaps it was even a figment of the other Olivia's imagination.

It would be untrue to say, "I dreamed you."
I never believed such beauty ever really
existed.

22

Olivia

It's true that I had much too much to drink, but I felt really happy. I couldn't remember ever being so happy. I looked up into Marlow's face and I could hardly believe I had found such a perfectly gorgeous man. I felt so lucky and so blessed. I leaned on Marlow, his body warm and sheltering as an ancient oak, as we waited to get our coats. Outside, he stopped and pulled my collar up. And I looked up at him and the rest of the world just fell away. It was just him and me. There was so much I didn't know about him. The world was our oyster.

In the taxi, on the way to his flat, I tried to keep it light.

'I saw a documentary yesterday about a hypnotist,' I told him.

'Oh yeah?'

'Yes, this hypnotist had been asked to cure a football team of their smoking habit. All he did was touch their foreheads and they were dropping on the ground like flies. Minutes later they woke up cured of all need to smoke. And when he lit a cigarette and gave it to them they were physically sick from it.' I paused. 'The hypnotist looked suspiciously like you.'

He grinned. 'Yeah, that was me.'

'How come you can't do that with me then?'

'That's TV for you—high impact editing. It took me hours to get those guys down.'

I touched his hand. 'I hardly know anything about you.'

He grasped my hand firmly. 'What do you want to know?'

'I don't know.' I shrugged. 'Do you have family?'

'Yes, I still have family back home. I just don't see them anymore.'

'Why?'

He sighed. 'It was a mistake on my part to cut them off. I shouldn't have. They were just trying to help. Everybody was trying to help. They just didn't know how to.'

'You can always make up.'

He grasped my hand tightly. 'I will. I see now how wrong I was. I was in pain so I struck out at those that were closest to me.'

I blinked. Just as he had spoken I'd had a flashback. I looked at him in wonder. 'I just remembered something.'

He looked worried. 'What?'

'I remembered that I had a pet peacock called Andrew. He used to fly up to my room and peck on the lead windows and when he saw that I was awake he used to fly back down and wait for me to come downstairs. And we would walk in the garden, my arm around his neck.' I turned back to him and laughed. I felt excited about that memory. It was the first clear memory I had had since leaving the hospital.

I remembered Dr. Greenhalgh saying, *'Memories are never truly gone. They prowl waiting for a gap in the mind's door. When the gap is found they leap out from the unknown into the known.'*

'Do you think my memories are returning?' I asked Marlow.

'Maybe,' he said, so softly I almost didn't hear it.

'You don't sound happy about it.'

'I don't want you to get your hopes up. They could never return, Olivia.'

When we got to his place, he disappeared into the bathroom and I took a tiny bottle out of my purse and put it on the dining table. Then I took all my clothes off and, sitting on the table, waited for him.

I had a surprise for Dr. Kane.

Marlow

When I found her she was sitting on my dining table totally naked. While watching me

she opened her legs wide. Then she picked up a little glass container that she must have brought with her and dipped her fingers into it. It was half filled with white powder.

I frowned. What the...?

She smeared the white powder all over her pussy, carefully getting it into all the folds and cracks and cervices. Then she pushed her white-coated finger in.

I stared at her in shock. I didn't want to get into drugs. That was one slippery slope I didn't want to test, but fuck me, I was bursting my pants to fuck her. There was something so damn hot about a woman meticulously rubbing her own sex with an unknown substance.

'Is that what I think it is?' I asked carefully.

She raised her eyebrows flirtatiously. 'What do you think it is?'

'Cocaine,' I replied sternly. I wanted her pussy. I fucking wanted to devour her, but no way was I getting into that shit. She was going straight into the shower before I stuck my tongue into that delicious hole of hers.

She shook her head slowly. 'Nope. It's not coke. Come and see what it is.'

I frowned suspiciously.

'Go on, be a devil,' she urged.

I walked up to her. She opened her legs a fraction more and pushed her groin upwards so her white-smeared flesh begged to be eaten or fucked senseless.

I looked into her knowing, laughing eyes and I knew. I was as safe as a baby at its mother's breast. I pushed her down on the table and swooped on her sex.

Sugar.

Powdered fucking sugar.

But hey! What a fucking turn-on. She had deliberately added the illegal forbidden element into an already explosive mix. I licked every last bit of it. Swirling my tongue around her clit and flicking the tiny white stem until she writhed in ecstasy.

I remembered that she had sneaked some up into her, too. I pushed my tongue as deep as it would go and licked it all out. And when it was all gone and only the tasty taste of her remained I clamped my mouth over her clit and I gave her what for. I sucked and sucked and sucked until she screamed and tried to push my head away, but still I did not stop.

That'll teach her—smearing sugar all over her pussy!

And lo and behold she came again. By the time I laid her on the bed she was utterly spent so I fucked her and spilled my drink inside her. I fell asleep with my arm curled around her waist. It was a good feeling. My last thought was I'm gonna make her mine.

Olivia

I didn't know what had woken me up, but suddenly I was wide awake. And the only thing in my head was the expression on Marlow's face when he said that perhaps my memories would never return. Even though I was drunk I had felt it. He didn't want my memories to return. There was something in my past that was so awful that he did not want me to access it.

His palm was spread on my stomach. Very slowly I lifted it and as quietly and as gently as I could I slid out from under it. I rolled and stopped, then rolled again and then slowly dropped my feet to the ground. Making as little movements as possible I got out of bed and left the room. By the mirror I saw the bunch of keys. I had one chance to do it tonight. He had left all the equipment in the soundproof room and walked out after my session, which meant that my recordings would be easy to access.

I dressed quickly and, closing myself in the kitchen, I called the minicab company I used. I whispered the address and told them to text me when they were outside. Then I switched the ringer off and kept the phone in my hand. Less than ten minutes later my mobile vibrated in my hand. I took the keys and carefully opening the front door walked down the steps and went out into the night.

The night was chilly, and the sky midnight blue with not a star in sight.

23

Olivia

It was not a long drive to Marlow's office, but it felt like an awfully long time. I was so nervous I dropped the money while I was trying to pay the taxi driver and had to scramble around on the taxi floor for it.

He was a decent sort of fellow.

'You sure you don't want me to wait until you get in your door? Can't be too careful these days.'

'I'm sure I'll be all right,' I said.

After he drove off I wondered if I should have let him wait for me. The street was completely deserted and eerily quiet and the first few keys were not the right ones.

I tried all the bigger keys in the door until the lock turned. Relieved, I swung the door open and quickly closed it firmly behind me. The alarm started bleeping. Beryl had given me the code the last time she slipped me in so I keyed it in. The bleeping stopped. I did not switch on any lights. The only illumination came from the emergency lights on the stair landings, but it was enough. I felt like a thief as I ran lightly up the wooden stairs. On my third try I found the key to Marlow's office. I went in and stood in the shadowy space. Some part of me was afraid of what I was about to do.

But for so long now the curious flashes, hints and impressions had come, catching me unawares and sometimes startling me. My deeper mind was conscious of some shadow, some vague unrest that needed to be let out from my past and into my future. I drifted in the shadows, slowly. Like a ghost, letting my fingers trail along the wall, the desk, the gray cabinet. My breath misted in front of me.

I needed to do this. I was changing. Every day I was becoming more and more of something, but until I had all the elusive memories, everything that belonged to me, I could never really be me. Everything always came back to my lost memories. It was important. And I wanted them back. Whatever they may be, they were mine.

I wandered into the soundproof room. It was completely dark. I turned on a light and went up to the recording equipment. I was nervous and jittery. I stood back and stared at it. I ran my finger along the smooth black panel. It felt forbidden and dangerous. A screen lit up. At the top left-hand corner it said:

Swanson, Olivia.

The buttons were easy enough to figure out. All my sessions were dated and could be accessed at the press of a button. I touched the square that said Session 1.

The screen filled with white noise. And then a night-vision image of Marlow and me popped onto the screen, and suddenly I felt excited. My stomach was clenched with nervous energy. Finally. Finally I was going to meet my past.

I went back to the chair where Marlow always sat and I watched myself. At first it was shocking to see myself without any will, a puppet. But then my body plunged with shock and I leaned forward in a daze. Session after session after session I stared at the screen until it seemed to swirl before my eyes.

My own voice mocking me.

What? How can that be true? Me a prostitute? Ridiculous. The Invisible Society? I could not believe it. I refused to believe it. It must be that false memories syndrome. Yes, that was what it was. Daffy had been right all along. It was all a mistake to hypnotize me. And Marlow believed in this utter rot! I felt angry. Something solid and hard was in my belly.

In the recording Marlow was asking a hypnotized me, *'How many men are in the room?'*

'Twelve,' the strange me replied.

'Oh my God!' My voice was a gasp. How could he believe that about me? Me a whore? Why? Why would I do that? I didn't need money. It was all so silly it was laughable. I closed my eyes and saw myself sitting in the red and gilt chair wearing nothing but the shiny black boots. And the false eyelashes. I snapped my eyes open. The image vanished. I was back in the clinical room with the night-vision recording still running. My head began to ache. I felt so confused. I should never have come here. I stood up to leave. I walked to the door and then I heard myself say in that weird monotone, 'They're coming up the stairs.'

And suddenly I began to shake. Goose bumps spread along my skin like wildfire. Something swelled in my brain. I shook my head. No. No. I walked out of the soundproof room but I could still hear my own voice. I walked to the door. No. No. I opened the door. What had they done to me? Oh my God! I couldn't see properly. My eyes were filled with tears. I tried to blink them away, but more arrived. I reached the top of the stairs and put my foot down and missed, and in that second while my arms were pin-wheeling and I was falling, those seconds before my flailing hands caught the banister, I had a flashback.

It was almost like an electric shock. The sounds were too loud, the colors too bright. The images needle sharp. I was not allowed to be an observer. I was sucked into it. It felt more real than the room I had been sitting in, the cold leather of the chair against the backs of my legs, the cold hard feel of the banister, the pain on my knee from where it had knocked the edge of the wall, the cold of the stair under my bare foot, where I had lost my shoe.

I was not watching the flashback.

I was *living* it.

I was walking down the corridor of my recurring dreams. It was cold. Only now I recognized it clearly as the east wing of Marlborough Hall. That was where Mummy and I lived. I had woken up frightened with a strange dream of crows calling to me and I was going to see Mummy. As I walked I became more and more frightened. I reached Mummy's door and I turned the knob and I saw it.

I saw Ivana. And she saw me. Slowly she turned her head and looked at me. She seemed unhurried. She was holding a pillow over Mummy's head and her eyes—her eyes were chilly. She hated me. I stared, astonished. I didn't know what to do. Mummy's hands were clawed on the sheets. I couldn't even scream. She left Mummy and she started to walk toward me. And I turned around and ran. I ran to the end of the corridor toward the stairs. She reached the stairs at the same time as I did.

I felt her hands push me and then I was falling. I fell and fell and fell. Until the floor opened up beneath me and everything collapsed into a black hole, the stairs, the pain, the sound of Blanca screaming my name from the direction of the kitchen, my memories, all disappeared into it.

For a while I could not catch my breath and then I doubled over and vomited. The smell horrified me. I grasped the banister and ran down the stairs of Marlow's office. I opened the door and ran into the street. I ran up it screaming. I wore no shoes, but I did not feel the cold.

Marlow

The scream was blood-curdling. The hairs at the back of my neck rose. That was her voice. I began to run in the direction of her scream. I found her up the road. Her feet were bare and dirty. She whirled around at my approach, her hands raised as if to strike. Under the street lamp her eyes were as wild and crazy as a blood-mad raptor. Her lips were almost blue in her startling white face. There was a bruise on one side of her cheek. She opened her mouth in a great roar and sprang at me. But not in attack.

She wanted to curl up in my arms.

I caught her, weak, defenseless and terrified, and squeezed her hard against my chest. She was trembling and her body was as cold as a corpse. I got her out of the road and onto the sidewalk.

'I've remembered. I know who the white owl is.' Her voice was a thin, high screech. She began to sob as if her heart was broken and would never again mend.

I felt waves of pity and anger wash into my chest simultaneously. I did not know what she had remembered, but I didn't care. I was not her hypnotist. I was her man. I didn't care what she had done in the past—she was my woman and I loved her with every fiber of my being. I'd die before I'd let anyone hurt her.

She'd come back to herself and that was enough. She was out of the labyrinth of her mind. The maze had not led her to the minotaur. It had brought her to me.

I stroked her hair tenderly.

'Do you know?' she asked.

I frowned. 'No,' I said. 'You never could go all the way.'

'It's too horrible to tell,' she whispered into my chest.

'It's all right. It's all right,' I repeated again and again.

She looked up at me, her eyes blurred with tears. I took my jacket off and put it over her shoulders. 'I'm taking you home,' I said.

24

Olivia

I tried to stand, but my knees gave way and I would have fallen to the ground if he had not caught me. He put his strong arms under my knees and back and carried me to his car.

In the car I turned my face away from him. The whole time he knew. I felt tainted and filled with self-loathing. Shame was like a thorn bush growing deep inside my chest. Stretching, blooming, willfully tearing, carelessly drawing blood.

I remembered his silky, seductive voice. 'You have escaped the cage. Your wings are stretched out. Now fly.'

Maybe one day I would thank him for showing me these things about myself. Not today. Today I was too cut up. I had believed that I belonged with him, you see. I had believed that I belonged to him. I was the tattoo on his body.

The journey seemed to be over very fast. He opened my side of the door and gathered me to him. He held me so close I could feel his heartbeat. As steady as a Swiss watch. He carried me up the stairs.

'You're cold,' he said. 'Let's get you in bed.'

'No, I need a shower. I'm dirty.'

'You're not dirty. You're the cleanest person I know.'

'I need a shower,' I said, my voice breaking.

He carried me straight into the shower. When he put me down I swayed slightly and he tightened his hold on my body. The tiles were cold under my feet. I shivered from the loss of his body warmth. He stripped me quickly. Goose bumps peppered my skin.

'I know. I know you're cold,' he murmured soothingly. Still holding onto me he leaned away from me. I heard the sound of water splashing and then he was gently guiding me under the hot stream. I sighed. Barely able to move I closed my eyes. He was still holding onto my forearms. Strength seeped from his hands into my skin. I felt safe. For the first time in a very long time I felt safe. Utterly safe.

Tears began to flow out of my eyes. I thought he wouldn't know. Not with the water rushing over my face, but he said softly, 'Don't cry, princess. No more tears for you. I'm here now.'

That only made me cry even harder. My body shuddered with sobs. He held me as I bawled my eyes out. I cried for ages until I was exhausted. I slumped onto his chest. He made a move. He was going to take me out.

'Soap. I'm still filthy,' I whispered.

He pressed me against his body. 'You're *not* filthy,' he snarled.

'Soap,' I breathed weakly.

His jaw was clenched tight but he leaned me against the tiles and reached for the soap. It smelt of apples. Clean. Fresh. Crisp. Everything I was not. With gentle circles he washed my soiled shoulders, my dirty neck, my gross arms, my foul forearms, my lusty hands, my unclean fingers. All those wicked men. I had let them all abuse me. I had been wet and sticky for their perverted desires. I had let them fuck me. I had let them come inside me. Grubby, grubby Olivia. I didn't deserve this clean, wonderful man.

Tenderly, he did my breasts, letting the bar slide over my nipple. I wanted to thrust forward, but I was too ashamed, too polluted to touch a man like him. The soap traveled across to my armpits, down to my ribs, my stomach, my hips.

When he reached the unspeakably mucky, disgusting area between my legs he began to slide the soap through the curls. Slowly he rubbed his hand on the mound until it lathered creamy and white. He gently cleaned between the creases. My thighs drifted open of their own accord. This was the part that reeked of all the other men. This was the dirtiest part. He must have understood because he spent more time washing it. When his palm made contact with my clit, the sensation was electric and I jumped with shock.

His hands moved down to my thighs, my calves, my feet, paying particular attention to my grimy soles. The water turned muddy. He turned me around and did my back and the stinking cleft between my buttocks. The nameless men had used me well. How had I not seen it? Slowly, he turned me around.

'Close your eyes.'

I did as he asked.

He washed my face and then my hair. I felt the slippery soapsuds slide softly down my body.

'Open your eyes.'

I looked at him.

'You're totally clean now,' he said softly.

I slid down the tiles and spread my knees wide.

'Wash me inside. It's the dirtiest place of all,' I said.

He hunkered down. His hair was wet and plastered to his body. His eyelashes were thick and black and his eyes were glittering with anger.

'You're clean inside, Olivia,' he said through clenched teeth.

'You don't understand. You have to wash me,' I begged.

'I'm sorry, baby. I'm so sorry for what they did to you. But you're not dirty.'

'You don't get it.'

'No, you don't get it. I don't care what you've done or how many men you've been with. It doesn't even matter to me if you enjoyed it. I don't give a flying fuck about any of those things. I just want you just as you are. You're clean, baby.'

I shuddered. I felt as if I was bleeding inside. All the things he had said—they meant nothing. I just knew I needed to be clean again. 'Please,' I begged.

The rigidness went out of him. An expression crossed his face. It could have been profound pity or even savage anguish. He closed his eyes for a second. When he opened them he was transformed. His eyes were like the weathered stony face of a mountain. It had stood its ground for centuries and it would remain unchanged and immovable for centuries more.

He rose up and soaped his fingers. He sat on his heels and tenderly inserted two soapy fingers inside. I gasped. I gasped at what we were doing. I gasped at that man. At his kindness. Surely he could not be mine. His eyes never faltered. Very gently he moved his fingers inside me, washing me clean. Then he pulled his fingers out and let the water pound the suds away before he put them back inside me. I watched the lather and all the mess of unclean fluids, mine and all the other men's, gush down the sinkhole. He did it until his hands came out clean. I saw that the pads of his fingers were beginning to crinkle.

'It's done,' he said softly.

I nodded. I placed my palms on the floor and tried to push myself up, but it seemed too great an effort. He grabbed me under my arms and pulled me up and leaned me against the tile.

'One last thing,' he said and went down on his haunches again. The space was so thick with steam his head seemed to rise out of clouds of white. Like being in a misty dream.

'Don't,' I objected, but my voice lacked strength.

'It's OK,' he said. 'I love you.'

He pulled apart my lower lips and leaning forward plunged his long, searing tongue as deeply into me as he could. Shocking heat exploded at my core, the ripples fanning out into my bloodstream. It was insane but at the edges of my consciousness was an instinct to want him, no matter what. I put my hands on his head, grabbed handfuls of his wet hair, and leaned my head back against the tiles.

Water flooded down over my face. I was so tired I felt floaty. My brain felt as though it was wrapped in cotton wool. *Crikey, what did he just say?* Surely I must have misheard him. *Silly Vivi, of course you misheard.* Something inside me broke at the thought.

What he was doing between my legs seemed to be happening to someone else. All the fire licking up my belly couldn't be happening to me. I closed my eyes as the water rained down on me and he covered my clit with his warm velvety mouth and began to suck. It felt so damn good. New blood began to pump into my tired, aching limbs. Desire began to course through my body. My nipples ached for the feel of his fingers.

I looked down at him.

The movement made his eyes flicker open. They were smoky with desire. He extended his tongue and teased and tortured the tip of my clit until I wanted to scream. I rubbed his face in my sex.

'I'm coming,' I warned breathlessly and he opened his mouth to receive all my juices. I slumped against the wall, limp and spent.

He shut off the water, dried me. I felt his cock, thick and full and unspent, brush against me. I should have done something for him, I thought vaguely as he carried me to his bed. The sheets smelt of lavender. I sat curled in his bathrobe while he dried my hair. Afterwards he fluffed the pillows and put me to bed. Empty and drained I lay on the pillow and looked up at him. He kissed the crown of my head over and over again, and each time he promised to take care of me until the day he died. Then he looked down at me with quiet strength until I fell into a deep sleep.

—You're the only thing I want to touch—

25

Olivia

For a moment after I opened my eyes, the next morning was just another day. I blinked at the plain white walls, the masculine chocolate curtains, and the light pouring in at the edges. Marlow's flat. I was naked between the scratchy sheets—mental note: go to Liberty's and get some proper cotton ones.

And then it came, tumbling, sliding, hurting. Rocking my world. Questions hurtling towards me like an avalanche.

Twelve men at a time!

An involuntary sob hit the back of my throat. I covered my eyes instinctively as if I could stop the ugly thoughts and images. I felt strong hands grip my wrists and pull my palms away from my eyes. Marlow was crouched in front of me, buck-naked, his eyes were shining. In the morning light he looked so brown and big and sturdy. So full of vigor. I gazed at him in awe. It was almost like being in a dream.

'I love you, Olivia,' he said softly, his voice as caressing as velvet. 'And there's not one fucking thing about you I'd change.'

I opened my mouth. He was so amazing, so kind. But how could he look at me as anything other than a prostitute. At that moment I just wanted to disappear. I felt so unworthy of him. Tears stung at the back of eyes.

'Not one fucking thing,' he repeated.

'But ... I ... was a whore,' I choked, tears rolling down my cheeks.

'Yeah, you were. Now tell me why I can't love you.'

I stared at him. I had no answer.

He smiled tenderly. 'You are beautiful, delicate and damaged, a terrifying combination to most people. They won't know how to love you. But I know.'

'But—'

'There is only one but.'

'What?' I whispered, suddenly frightened. Even the tears dried.

He gazed into my eyes. 'Do you still want to be a slave at the Invisible Society?'

I recoiled as if struck. Even the thought sickened me. 'No. Absolutely not.'

'Then there *is* no other 'but' to worry about, is there?' He lifted one shoulder in a shrug. 'I don't know if I would have fallen in love with that unhappy, pitiful woman who needed the toxic combination of sex and danger to get her rocks off that you were, before you lost your memory and had to start again. But I do know that I worship you as you are now. To me there is no other you. This is the real you. And this you is everything I could ever have dreamed of.'

'But I feel so ashamed of what I've done.'

'It's not your fault. You were just a child, an innocent, blameless child, when he twisted and over-sexualized you. What could you have done?'

I frowned. 'So you don't mind?'

'Mind?' he snarled. His jaw clenched and a vein beat at the side of his neck. 'I mind so much it burns. I want to kill that pervert who did that to you. And while I'm at it I want to chop off the dicks of all those bastards in that sick society' He shook his head. 'But I can't. So I won't let myself fester in hate, I'll just love you more.'

I licked my lips nervously. 'What if ... we're out and someone who has ... uh ... someone who knows what I have done comes up and says something nasty to you?'

'Look at me. Do I look like one of your lily-livered English toffs to you? I'm without my hat and boots, but I grew up on a ranch outback. We don't let nobody disrespect our women.'

'I'll only bring you down,' I muttered.

'Oh sweet child. You don't get it at all, do you? Until you came into my life I was staring at guilt in the bottom of a bottle of whiskey every night. I had nothing, nothing to live for.'

I was full of doubts, the inside of my head like a knotted rope. I could see the knots but I couldn't undo them. 'I'm afraid.'

'Of what?'

'The only thing I remembered last night was what happened on the day my mother died, but everything else I know only from what I heard in the recordings. I'm scared I will slowly start remembering more and more and I just don't want to remember any more of what I did in that horrible society.'

'If you remember something that upsets you, then you'll tell me about it, and we'll deal with it.'

'We?'

'Yes, we. You're the color of my blood, Olivia. What hurts you hurts me. There is no difference between your skin and mine.'

I sniffed.

'And after we have spoken about it you can keep the memory if you want, or we can hide it away. Up to you. OK?'

'OK.' I paused. 'But what if it is something unforgivable?'

'Everything is forgivable, my angel. There is no life for me without you.'

With a sudden jerk he yanked the duvet cover down my legs. My first reaction was a strange and unexpected one. A strangled gasp of horror ran out of my mouth while my hands flew to cover my breasts and my sex. I had become shockingly and painfully ashamed of my nakedness. I dropped my chin to my chest, my hair making a curtain for me hide to behind. My whole body shivered in the chill of the morning air.

For a few seconds he did nothing. Then he put a finger beneath my chin and lifted it up so I was forced to meet his eyes.

'Why are you hiding?' he asked.

I stared wordlessly at him.

'You're prefect,' he whispered.

His words tugged at my heart. He was reeling me in as surely as a fish caught on a hook. His finger traced the line of my jaw and lingered on its way down my throat.

'So fucking perfect...' He smiled suddenly, a triumphant, possessive smile. '... that I claim you.'

I heard the fierce pleasure in his voice. He removed his finger and my skin tingled where it had been.

'All fucking mine. Every last inch. Today I brand you as my sole property. From this day forth you will be only mine. No one other may look, touch or enter what is now mine.' He paused. 'Who do you belong to woman?'

'You,' I whispered hoarsely.

He nodded. 'Good. Place your hands behind your head.' It was a definite command not a request.

My eyes popped open with surprise. I opened my mouth to object, but no words came. Only a strange excitement coursing through my blood. I felt hot and shivery at the same time. His eyes were dark, commanding, full of lust and utterly mesmerizing. I couldn't take my eyes off him. Slowly my hands left my breasts and the triangle of hair between my legs, and linked behind my head.

He let his gaze lazily rake down my body. I swallowed hard. I had never felt so exposed or spread open before.

'Are you wet?' he asked, already knowing the answer.

'Yes,' I admitted and felt ashamed of my sexuality, my wantonness, my lack of decorum, and the desperation with which I wanted him. I just wanted to hide away from him and the knowledge of myself. I closed my eyes.

'Open your eyes, Olivia.' His voice low and deep: demanding.

I obeyed.

'Spread your legs so I can see the soft sweet flesh of my cunt.' He spoke softly, but his eyes flashed possessively.

I bit my lip and stared into his molten eyes. They were devouring me. There was longing there. Intense longing. No one had ever looked at me like that. My clit responded instantly, throbbing violently, wanting, begging. Slowly, I opened my thighs.

His eyes dropped to my sex.

'Wider,' he commanded.

Tingling waves radiated through me, settling in my core, making me feel as if I was wax, melting under the heat of his gaze. The simple unadorned truth was I wanted to be filled. I needed him to fix the ache. I was so ready for his cock. My legs inched apart, the soles of my feet dragging, the sheet tangled around one ankle a delicious ache between my legs, and a wicked thrill running up my spine. That first instinct to cover myself was completely gone. Now I wanted him to watch me. I wanted to see his eyes shining and greedy for what he had claimed as his.

I put on a little show. I arched my back so my breasts thrust forward, the tips aching for his mouth, his teeth, his fingers, anything.

A low growl rumbled in his throat.

When I could spread no further his eyes roved over my body proprietarily, with ownership, the way a man would look at a prized horse or a painting he had fought hard to acquire at an auction. 'That's better,' he said and reaching out grazed his fingers slowly along my inner-thigh. His eyes never left mine. I was so wet I was afraid I was dripping onto his sheet.

He brushed his fingers in an upward motion through the slick, swollen folds of my sex. A gasp escaped me. '.' Gently his thumb began to circle my clit and I drew a shuddering breath. 'It's true,' he said huskily, 'your pussy is like a very, very ripe and juicy fruit and I could fuck it all day and all night long. And it is also true I wanted to fuck you from the moment you walked into my office, no, scrap that, from the moment, Beryl showed me a picture of you on the Internet.

And it's true that due to the... ah ... complicated nature of our relationship I've done nothing so far, but fuck you but, don't for a moment think you're not going to get the flowers, the chocolates, the cinema, the dinner dates, and the whole fucking shebang.'

All the while his thumb never stopped massaging.

'We're going to start over,' he said, and casually pushed a finger into me.

I moaned.

He leaned forward and took a nipple in his warm mouth. 'Oh,' I cried. He sucked it while his fingers played with my pussy.

He raised his head, his face so sincere it almost made me want to cry. 'You're not in the limbo of the past. You're with me now. You're my woman. My baby. And nothing from the past can change that. From now on you are flying under my wings. Anybody who wants to hurt you has to go through me first. Do you understand that?'

'Yes,' I whispered, staring transfixed at his gorgeous face.

'I'd kiss you all over, but that wouldn't be enough. I'd lick you all over, but that wouldn't be enough either.' He grinned suddenly. 'I'll just have to fuck you until you faint.'

And he grabbed me, his thumbs pressing into the creases where my thighs began and the rest of his large palms curled underneath my buttocks, and jerked me forward. I squealed with the suddenness of his actions.

In a smooth move of his big, sturdy body, he aligned his thick, long cock with my entrance.

'I love you, Marlow Kane,' I said.

For a second he didn't move, just froze as if made of stone.

'I know that,' he said hoarsely, and drove himself deep inside me. He stilled and waited until my muscles stretched and adjusted to his size. When I exhaled with pleasure he began to thrust, his strong hands gripping my flesh so hard I knew he would leave bruises in the shape of his fingerprints. But I wanted him to mark me. It is a primal thing to darken the skin of the one that belongs to you. When he sees the marks he will know: I am his. When I see the marks I will know: I am his.

Pinned under his big sturdy body with his cock deeply embedded inside me, I looked him in the eye and urged, 'Harder.'

His cock slammed into me.

'Yes,' I screamed.

The thrusts were savage and relentless. His body slapped at my clit. When I started to feel the edges of an orgasm a smothered cry escaped my lips. Above me his body became solid. I gripped the hard muscles of his upper-arms and we exploded at the same moment. He came over and over inside me, the eruptions rocking us both. Finally it was over. Our foreheads touched, our breathing hot and heavy.

'I really, really, really, really love it when you wear me at the end of your cock, Marlow Kane,' I whispered shyly.

He grinned. 'And I'm gonna fill you so full of my cum it's going to be dripping out of you for days.'

Hours later I stared up at him. 'You know who the white owl is, don't you?'

His face changed. 'I don't for sure, but I can guess.'

Incredibly curious, I asked, 'How did you guess?'

'Because the first law of war is to keep your friends close and your enemies even closer.'

I thought of all her silky lies. The betrayal was like a wound in my chest. I shook my head. Then another thought, totally unrelated, struck me: my missing shiny black stiletto boots. 'My God! She knew I was a ...,' I paused it was hard to say the word, '... a prostitute.'

'Why do you say that?'

'Because she secretly went to my flat and removed everything that could have acted as a

 233

trigger to remind me of that part of my life. I don't know what her plan was, but I think she meant to use you to confuse me. All my memories would have been seen as too preposterous to be real. God! I can't believe how devious and insidious she is! I've been so stupid. I never guessed. Not for a moment.'

'Don't be so hard on yourself, Olivia. You were fooled by a consummate actress,' he consoled.

'She not just a consummate actress she's also a murderer,' I spat out furiously.

He scowled. 'Murderer?'

'She killed my mother. I saw her. I saw her smother Mummy with a pillow.' My voice wobbled with the memory of that night.

Something flashed in his eyes. 'But that doesn't make sense. I thought your mother was dying. Why not just wait it out?'

He was right. Why? Why would she take the risk? Then it hit me.

'Daffy. She was already sleeping with my father and pregnant with Daffy. She didn't want her child to be a bastard. She was hoping it would be a boy who could inherit the title and estate. Daffy was born seven months after my mother died, and Ivana claimed it was premature. Of course, everybody knew, but no one said anything.'

I laughed suddenly, a humorless, joyless sound.

'And she's been French kissing karma ever since. She found out after Daffy was born that she couldn't have any more children. She could not produce a male heir for my father'

'What will you do?'

'I want to punish her. I want her to suffer.'

26

Olivia

My father was watching a race on the box. He had money on Penny Turns Up Again. I walked up to him.

'Daddy,' I called.

He glanced up impatiently. 'Hello, princess!'

'Daddy, I've remembered some of my past.'

'Come in then,' he said reluctantly. He did not switch off the TV, but muted it to indicate he did not expect me to stay long.

I sat down on the armchair next to him, smoothed my skirt over my legs and looked him in the eye. 'I remembered the day Mummy died.'

He stared at me uncomfortably. Poor Daddy. He had a horror of emotional scenes. Was there any point telling him? Yes. Mummy deserved that. Everything else had been taken away from her.

He cleared his throat. 'What did you remember, ducky?'

'I woke up in the night because I had a bad dream and I went to Mummy's room. I opened the door and Ivana was there. She was suffocating Mummy with a pillow.'

My father's eyes bulged with incredulity. 'Poppycock!' he blurted out. 'Poppycock!' he said again. His face became red with anger. 'It's that half-wit American hypnotist who has put these nonsensical ideas into your head.'

'Dr. Kane didn't do any such thing,' I said calmly.

He looked at me with disappointment. 'You do Ivana a great injustice. How could you even dream of spouting such lies about her after she has treated you as if you were her own.'

'She wanted Mummy out of the way so she could marry you.'

He shook his head. 'I can't believe that you could even think such a thing. What are you saying? Think about it. Ivana took excellent care of your mother. Your mother was genuinely fond of her.'

'Ivana was wearing a green dress with a yellow belt and the big round buttons on her dress were made of the same material as her dress.'

My father's mouth dropped open. We stared at each other. The tongue can conceal the truth but never the eyes. In those seconds the unguarded truth leapt up from the depths of his soul and shone momentarily in his eyes, and it was all over. He was caught as surely as a fish on a hook.

He dropped his eyes. 'I can't do without her, ducky. She takes care of everything...the house...the estate...our schedule.... I couldn't do without her.'

I nodded. 'I knew you'd say that, but I had to tell you, for Mummy's sake.'

He nodded, still looking at the ground.

'I'd better push off then.' I stood up and began to walk to the door.

'Princess?'

I turned around. His shoulders were slumped. He looked crushed. I pitied him then.

'You won't be unkind, will you?'

'Of course not.'

'You won't tell anyone?'

'Who'd believe me, Daddy? The mad stepdaughter. They would simply call it false memory. It was why she sent me to Dr. Kane in the first place. She knew I was beginning to remember things and this way all my memories could be discredited.' I smiled. 'You've underestimated Mummy's nurse, Daddy. She's managed us all perfectly.'

He gawped at me. I had never seen my father look so agonized or lost. He shook his head as if to reject what I was saying.

'She picked Dr. Kane precisely because she knew he was disgraced and she found out that he had a drinking problem. If he failed she could say it was because he was a drunk, if he was successful she could claim the process was faulty.'

My father shifted, his eyes pleading. 'You will understand that this is all very difficult for me? Your mother is gone and I...um...am very fond of Poppe—her.'

In the end my father could always be relied on to retreat into self-interest. Above all else, what was good for William Elliot Swanson.

'I understand perfectly,' I said and went to walk away again.

'Wait.'

I turned once more.

'I'm issuing a new Letters Patent stating that the eldest daughter may inherit both the title and the estate.'

I smiled sadly. 'I don't want it. Give it to Jacobi. Make his mother happy.'

He stood up and put his hand out in an awkward pleading gesture. 'Don't break this family up. That's all I beg of you.'

I began to walk.

My father cried out urgently. 'Please, Vivi.'

And I turned around and stared. He was out of his chair. A solitary tear was rolling down his cheek. I had never seen him cry before. I knew that single tear betraying his terrible pain had cost him his pride. Perhaps he had a great and pure love for her, after all.

'I won't harm you, Daddy. I love you,' I said softly and walked out of Marlborough Hall. When I reached the car I turned and looked up at the second floor bedroom. Ivana was watching me. In the gloom of the window she looked pale and insubstantial as a ghost. We stared at each other for a few moments. She did not wave and neither did I.

We both knew the truth. She had planned and schemed and lied and stolen and murdered, but there was no need to punish her. Her real tragedy was being stuck in a loveless marriage. Being married to a man so far inferior in intellect to her that he bored her stiff each day from the moment he opened his eyes in the morning.

I had seen it in her eyes many times—the desire for men other than my father—but she controlled it with an iron will. She had chosen the splendor of a public life and the envy of her friends without the true and lasting joy of inner satisfaction, but she deeply resented having to make that choice.

The weak morning sun was shining down on Marlborough Hall. It always looked its best on a sunny day. I turned away and got into my car and drove away without looking back. I would miss my conservatory, but otherwise there was nothing I would wish I had not left behind.

Soon it would be spring. And then summer.

27

Ivana

I stood at the window and looked at my reflection in the window. I was wearing a cream silk and wool dress. Cream suited my dark hair and pale coloring. Beyond my ghostly reflection lay the beautifully manicured gardens. Soon Dr. Kane will be here. My husband wanted to join me in the meeting but I dissuaded him. It was far better that I alone handle this matter.

Anyway, it was a relief to send him away to the stables. Last night I had to do all those things that I had not done for a very long time. I had almost forgotten how dreadfully white, flabby and sweaty he could get when he had to do the deed. Like a sack of wet sand he had puffed and panted on top of me while I pretended to enjoy it. I even took his shriveled, red penis into my mouth.

I stilled the shudder of disgust that ran through me and took a deep breath. There was a price to pay for everything. This house, the envy of all the people I knew, the glow of being recognized and treated as someone important, all of it had to be paid for. He was basking in the glow of our renewed passion this morning. I reinstated my power. So it was worth it.

I put him at the back of my mind. He was not important now. I watched Dr. Kane's car drive up. Inside me a serpent twisted and spewed its poison into my veins. The effect of its acid was immediate. My hands started to tremble. I clenched them into hard fists.

God, I hated that bitch. How I hated her.

She was supposed to die in that car accident. Anyone else would have just given up and died, but her? Noooo. Like an unwanted, ugly weed she sprouted up again. And now she was setting roots, becoming strong. Worse, she found a man to champion her. I had underestimated the cunningness of my step-daughter. The cheap little whore had done what cheap little whores do. Opened her legs and ensnared him. Now he was hers to bid.

The venom bubbled. It felt as if it was eating me up from inside.

I gritted my teeth.

What an awful miscalculation it had been to send her to him. How I regretted it. It kept me awake all night knowing that it was I who had arranged their meeting. I should have done my homework better. I should never have picked a man who was so physically beautiful, a man even I could have loved. I thought tragedy had felled him, made him an irredeemable shadow of himself, but I was wrong.

I remembered too late what my mother had told me. She said that all men could be described as boxes of goodies hanging on strings from a tree branch. There were three types of boxes. Empty, nearly empty and full. It was very easy to recognize the nearly empty boxes. They rattled a lot. They were always showing off, telling you how much money they earned or what a good lovers they were. The problem was distinguishing between the empty boxes and the full boxes since they both spoke very little.

I thought Dr. Kane was an empty box. But I was wrong. He was the full box my mother had told me about.

I heard the doorbell ring.

If only the little bitch had died in the accident. I closed my eyes and took a long calming breath. I was not beaten. All was not lost. I was resourceful. I could handle Dr. Kane. I could always handle a man. All men are susceptible to me.

She is not as beautiful as you. But the reflection of my face in the glass pane was marred with a frown. The truth was I was not sure how to mould him to my wishes.

He stood apart from other men. I saw it for myself at the dinner when I purposely invited the proudest and most caustic members of our set. And they did what I knew they would—deliberately set out to make him feel small and insignificant. But their veiled insults and disparaging comments were useless. He cared nothing for their good opinion.

Not only did he not recognize them as his betters, he refused to obey the social etiquette set by them. Instead he made his own rules without fear of what society thought of him. Men who will not be bullied by the artificial rules of society are more dangerous than men with knives. For they cannot be controlled.

And such a man was now my enemy. I did not want him as my enemy, but he was my foe, as surely as I was Olivia's.

Marlow

She stood when a servant showed me into her drawing room. She was dressed in a way that accentuated her fine figure and her hair was loose around her shoulders. Her face was perfectly made.

'Hello Dr. Kane,' she said with just the right amount of warmth.

'Lady Swanson,' I greeted with the slightest emphasis on the word Lady.

She looked at me sharply, but her voice was honey. 'Can I get you a drink?'

She was relying heavily on the assumption that I was a drunk. Well... first mistake. 'No thank you,' I refused. 'This is not a social call.'

'You won't mind if I have one,' she said and ordered a glass of brandy from her footman.

The door closed quietly behind him.

'Will you have a seat?'

'I won't be staying long enough to bother.'

She straightened. 'Well, we might as well get it over with it.'

'I'm marrying Olivia and I've come to tell you to arrange the biggest most fantastic wedding for her.'

A slow smile hit her face. 'Your slip is showing. You're not supposed to be so eager for the money. A less obvious approach would surely stand you in better stead.'

With my eyes fixed on her I took a step forward. I saw instantly that she was flustered. But oh how hard she forced herself to stand her ground. I took another step and I saw her swallow. So I closed the distance some more.

'Don't come any closer,' she blurted out.

I smiled. Slow. She knew me not at all. 'Why Lady Swanson, your slip is showing. You're not supposed to look so guilty.'

She flushed. 'It's not true. Whatever my stepdaughter thinks she has remembered is simply not true.'

I raised an eyebrow.

She knew better than to carry on that line of defense. 'Nobody would believe such utter rot,' she said icily.

I smiled. 'It would appear you are better than the crowd you run with. *Everybody* would believe it. It has the ring truth to it, wouldn't you say? Besides when has the truth ever stopped a nice piece of gossip'

'You think I'm powerless. I could destroy that little prostitute in a minute. I've got pictures.'

I was not surprised. I had expected no less, but she had more to lose than me. 'Yes, I was coming to that. You use your pictures and I'll use mine.'

Her eyes narrowed. 'What have you got?' she challenged, Her accent was no longer the stiff upper-lip drawl, but hard and nasal. It betrayed her real roots. She was from the East End of London.

'What's most precious to you?' I asked softly.

Her face contorted into an ugly mask. 'You wouldn't dare,' she spat.

'You met me in my hypnotist guise so you think I am civilized like you. I'm not. When you think of me, Lady Swanson, think of a bear. A grizzly bear. Better still think of me as a mama bear.' I paused and looked hard at her. 'If I catch you trying to undermine or hurt Olivia in any way at all, even if it is just a glance, I promise you I'll hurt him. Don't forget how easy it is to get him in one of those anonymous clubs he goes to all dolled-up as a woman.'

She went still. 'Is that a threat?'

'It's a prediction, but if it takes a threat to help you understand how serious I am then take it as such.'

There was a soft knock on the door. The footman came in with a tray and walked up to her. She snatched it off the tray and took a large gulp. The door closed again.

'What do you want?' she asked briskly.

'I want Olivia to have the wedding of her dreams. The whole works. The dress, the veil, the church, the bridesmaids, the flowers. Only you know her well enough to do that for me.'

'What else?' she asked tightly.

'I want to know where Tom your former gardener is?'

'Tom Hardy? He died sometime ago. Cancer, I believe.'

'Lucky him,' I said quietly

Something passed through her eyes. It was gone in a flash but I caught it.

I looked at her in shock. 'You knew, didn't you?'

'Knew what?' she asked defiantly.

I felt rage curling in my stomach. 'What kind of woman are you? You let him abuse a defenceless child.'

She swallowed. 'I don't know what lies she told you, but I had nothing to do with anything that happened between her and Tom.'

'But you protected your own daughter

'I'm not responsible for her,' she shouted.

People like her made me sick. 'The good news is I'll be taking Olivia back to America with me. So you'll hardly have to see her again, but I will bring her back as often as she wants and I want her to have a nice house here in London. I expect you and your husband to take care of that for her.'

She nodded. A gust of envy blew across her face. 'You're taking her away?'

'Yes, I'm going back to the States. I'm returning to the practice of neurology.'

'I see.'

'There's one more thing I want Olivia to have. And it's got to be a surprise.'

'What is it?' she asked warily

So I told her.

Always forgive your enemies. Nothing annoys
them so much.

—Oscar Wilde

Epilogue

Olivia

My wedding was a grand society affair, organized and perfectly executed by Ivana. No, it was not awkward. It was a great triumph. Everybody said so. Anybody looking in could only have envied our family, our beauty, our good fortune, our wealth, our happiness. They would have seen a proud father, a beautiful, polished, charming, utterly devoted stepmother and a bride who looked adoringly up at her bridegroom as if he was God on earth. Only the bride's adoring gaze for her new bridegroom as if he was God on earth was not an act.

The thing I remember most was walking into the church and seeing Marlow in his perfectly matched morning suit. He was watching me, every inch of me. There was no smile, no silently mouthed words of encouragement, no self-conscious gesture of love, just an intense look that said, I'm here, I've got your back. You'll never again be anything but precious.

My step faltered and my hand tightened on my father's arm. I felt him look down on me. I glanced up at him. His face was the perfect parody of the proud father. He had not taken care of me, but today he was giving me away to someone who would.

I took my gaze back to Marlow. He had not moved. He stood as still as a statue, his hands by his sides and I was reminded of my first impression of him, a slow-talking, gun-slinger on a dusty street at high noon, ready on the draw. Tense, alert and bristling with concentration. I stared at him and suddenly there was no one else in the church except him and me. As I drew in an exhilarating breath, I knew: I was safe forever.

And then I remember the kiss. Oh, the kiss. It was the most beautiful thing that had ever happened to me. After that it became a bit of happy blur. His hand on the small of my back, rose petals confetti, well-wishers, music, delicious food, cutting an eight-tiered cake, champagne...

There were speeches too. I don't remember any of them, of course. Only Marlow's. When he looked into my eyes in front of all the people who had tried to hurt me the most and said, 'I was not a man. I was a shell until you walked into my office.'

I had to blink back the stinging tears not only because that was exactly how I felt. I, too, had been a shell until I walked into his office. But because of a sense of triumph and vindication: none of *you succeeded in destroying me.*

Daffy came to kiss my cheek after the reception. 'You won the lottery. Don't spend it all at the races,' she said and laughed

I stared at her. *Et tu, Brute?* But the knowledge didn't hurt. I *had* won the lottery and I had absolutely no intention of squandering any of it at the races.

My father and Ivana had a surprise present for me—a house in Belgravia. Marlow was in on it, of course. We were driven up to it in a carriage. It was white stucco fronted with a columned entrance and a glossy black door. We went up the stairs. He took out a silk scarf.

'What?' I asked with a laugh.

'Turn around,' he said.

Still laughing I turned around and he tied the scarf over my eyes.

I stayed turned away from him while I heard him put the key in the door, turn the lock, then felt his strong hands come around me and I was airborne and giggling. He carried me laughing over the threshold and did not put me down straightaway. He did not even take me up the stairs to the bedroom, which I had expected him to do. Instead he walked in what appeared to my blindfolded senses to be a straight line, heading to the back of the house. I held onto his neck and nestled in the curve of his throat.

At that moment I was the happiest woman on earth.

He set me down, and I felt him move to the back of me. Even before he untied the scarf tears were already rolling down my face. I smelt them, you see. I smelt them the way a mother recognizes the scent of her newborn baby. The scarf fell away from my eyes and I gasped. My eyes moved from one child to another, to yet another. Every single one of them had made the journey back to me. All my babies had come to live with me. I turned around with shining eyes.

'Thank you, my love.' My voice was a shaky whisper.

He looked down at me with such love that heat flared in my chest.

'I can't take any of the credit. I wanted to ask your father's gardener to recreate your happy place here, but Ivana insisted that we move the entire contents of the conservatory. She's even sorted out a gardener to take care of it when we are not around.'

'Yes, dear Ivana,' I said sarcastically.

'You're so beautiful,' he said softly, refusing to take the bait. He once told me, as hateful as Ivana was, he could never be anything but grateful to her. She had unwittingly led him into his most fabulous dream.

'Oh yeah?' I said, imitating his accent.

'Yeah,' he said, all macho and gorgeous.

He slanted his eyes down to me. 'Well, aren't you craving to water the plants? Or something?'

I grinned. 'I'm craving something. See if you can guess.'

He laughed. 'That's too fucking easy,' he said as he went behind me and started unzipping my dress.

'Be careful with that. I'm saving this dress for my daughter,' I warned, my pulse humming under my skin.

'Our daughter,' he whispered in my ear. 'Our daughter. Our son. Our family.' I felt his mouth settle on my nape light as a butterfly.

I closed my eyes, happy, so unbelievably happy. This is my revenge, Ivana. To see me ecstatically happy. I tilted my head slightly. His eyes were directed down at the zip, his lashes casting a shadow on his cheek, and my breath caught at the beauty of the man. I took a mental photograph. I wanted to remember him like this forever.

'Now I think about it, don't worry about the dress. I hear they have a really good dry-cleaners in Belgravia.'

His laughter was muffled against my flesh. It mingled with the sound of my dress falling on the gray slate tiles. If they couldn't save it, she could jolly well buy her own.

Coming next...

SEXY BEAST

GEORGIA LE CARRE

The Mouse On The Bar Room Floor

Some Guinness was spilled on the bar room
floor
When the pub was shut for the night.
Out of his hole crept a wee brown mouse
And, in the pale moonlight,
He lapped up the frothy brew from the floor,
Then back on his haunches he sat.
And all night long you could hear him roar,
'Bring on the goddamn cat!'

—An Irish Tall Tale

ONE

Layla

Love is when a girl puts on perfume and a boy puts on shaving cologne and they go out and smell each other.

—Karl, Age 5

'**W**hat are you standing there for? Go use the upstairs bathroom,' Ria said, when she spotted me at the end of the queue to use the downstairs cloakroom.

She was right. The queue *was* long. 'I'll just use the portaloo outside,' I said.

'Don't be so silly. There's a humongous queue there, too.'

I bit my lip. Ria was BJ Pilkington's second cousin. We were in BJ Pilkington's house for a party he was throwing for my brother, Jake, and his new wife, Lily. And while I liked and socialized with Ria, BJ and I shared a stinging mutual dislike for each other.

In fact, I did not even want to come, but my mother had forced me to. 'It's in your brother's honor,' she had said in that displeased tone I knew not to disobey. 'It'd be ignorant not to, and God help me, I didn't bring you up to be ignorant.'

'Are you really sure it'll be OK?' I asked looking doubtfully at the long, curving, dark wood staircase. Nobody else seemed to be going up it. It was understood that the party was restricted to the four reception rooms downstairs.

'Of course,' she insisted confidently.

I gave it one last attempt. 'I don't even know where it is, and I don't really want to go wandering around by myself.'

'Come on, I'll show you,' she said, and, taking my hand, made for the stairs.

'Thanks, Ria,' I said, following her meekly. I did need the bathroom rather badly. At the top of the stairs I looked down and saw all the beautiful people dressed in their absolute finest. That's the thing with us travelers. We love our color. Peacocks we all are. There wasn't a plain black gown in sight. Ria took me down a corridor and half opened a door to a blue and white bathroom.

'See you downstairs,' she called brightly and walked away.

I used the toilet, washed my hands and stood in front of the mirror. My deeply auburn hair was straight and came down to the tips of my breasts. My eyebrows were straight like a man's and my eyes were blue. My nose was narrow, lips were generous and my jaw, I was convinced, was too square for a girl.

I was wearing a duck egg blue taffeta dress that I had designed and sewn myself. It had a tight bodice, a wide bow at the back of my waist, the ends of which trailed lower than the hem of my mid-thigh, honey boo boo skirt. Underneath were layers upon layers of gathered electric blue tulle and lace petticoats. Crinolines, my grandma used to call them.

I fluffed them up. I loved petticoats. In my opinion life was way too short not to wear petticoats that stick out from under your skirt. I reapplied my lipstick, pressed my lips and left the bathroom.

As I walked along the corridor I was suddenly and very strangely overcome by an irresistible curiosity. I wanted to open a door, just one, and see how BJ lived. I don't know why since I thought him an arrogant beast. But just for those seconds I wanted to see more than everyone downstairs saw. Oh! What the hell, just a quick look, I thought, and opened a door. It was plain and obviously just a spare bedroom. I closed it and opened another. It, too, had an unlived-in appearance. Again very plain. I tried another door.

Oh! Wow!

BJ!

I took a step forward, closed the door behind me, and leaned against it. And fuckin' stared. Two rooms had been knocked into one to make one massive space. The walls were black and the words 'No Fear' were painted in white using large Blackletter font. They glowed in the light from a real fire roaring in the fireplace. It was a long time since I had seen real logs.

A large chandelier hung from an iron hook in the ceiling that looked more like a meat hook. The bed was a huge wrought iron four-poster, obviously custom. It had deep red fleur de-lis patterned brocade curtains that had been gathered and held together by gold and black ties. On the bedside tables on either side of it were candelabras with real candles that had dripped wax onto the gilt handles.

Wow! This was what lay inside BJ.

His cold eyes hid the stage set of a seventeenth-century play. A dungeon! Or a torture chamber. But not in a horrible way. There was something irresistibly seductive about it. Like walking into his private world or looking into his soul. Dark and dangerous but I was strangely drawn to it.

I tried to imagine the room with the candelabras on. The candlelight dancing off the walls. My eyes moved to the bed and I saw me crushed under BJ's large body, the light making his muscles gleam. The image was so erotic I felt a flutter in my tummy, but it was also very disturbing.

I hated the man. And that was putting it politely.

And yet, here I was in his bedroom. A place I should never have been in. But unwilling to leave I walked to the middle of the room, my petticoats rustling, the heels of my shoes loud and echoing on the hardwood floor.

As if pulled by invisible hands I walked toward a dresser. It looked like an antique. In a trance I stroked the metal handle. It was cool, smooth, full of all the things it had seen for hundred of years, the squabbles, the trysts. *He* had touched this. His large hands had curled around it and pulled. A frisson of excitement ran over my skin. I pulled at the metal. It slid open with a whisper, smoothly, like it was on roller blades.

I stared at the contents.

Velvet boxes. Piled on top of one another. So many. I took one and opened it. A tiepin with a blue stone glittered up at me. I opened another. A tiepin with a black panther. It was obviously an old one. I opened another and froze. A tiepin that said 'Layla' in cursive writing. I lifted my head and looked at the mirror above the dresser. I looked different, strange, shocked. I shouldn't be here. This was wrong. I looked into my eyes.

What the fuck are you doing, Layla?

And then I did a strange thing. I'd *never* done anything like that before. I was a good girl. I'd always been a good girl. I took the

tiepin out of its box, opened my purse, and....
Oops... it fell in. I raised my head and saw my
reflection: it was no longer alone in the
mirror. BJ was standing in the doorway. His
big, powerful body filled it entirely.

Oh God!

Cold fear raced down my spine, my
pulse accelerated wildly and my mind went
into overdrive. Maybe he had not seen me lift
his tiepin. Perhaps I could just slip past him.
Or I could pretend I was lost. I did not know I
was in his bedroom. Maybe. Just maybe. I
turned around and faced him. Some men have
looks, other have charm, BJ had presence.
The moment he appeared in a room he owned
it. He changed the atmosphere the way a
grizzly coming into a room would.

He was wearing a silver hoop in his right
ear, a black shirt tucked into an army surplus
camouflage trousers and combat boots.
Straightening my back I began to walk toward
him. He remained still. He really was so damn
huge. My heart started to hammer inside my
chest. I was only five feet away. I could see his
eyes. They were deliberately blank. His mouth
was a forbidding line. For a moment I had the
impression of sexual tension. But of course,
that was a trick of my overawed emotions.

A foot away from him I stopped. The
scar on the top of his left cheek appeared alive
in the firelight. No man had ever looked more
dangerous or inhospitable.

'Sorry,' I said coolly. 'I got lost. I guess I better get back to the party.'

He did not move aside.

I clenched my handbag nervously. 'Will you please move?'

'You want to pass. Squeeze past,' he suggested, absolutely no expression on his face.

'How dare you? I'll call my brother.'

Something flashed in his eyes. I knew then that I'd made a mistake. I should have been more humble. It would have made my escape easier. He slipped his large hand into his trouser pocket and brought out a phone.

'That's a good idea.' His voice was silky and dangerous. 'Call him. Last time I looked he was with his pregnant wife. I believe your mother was sitting nearby, too. They can all rush up here to *my* bedroom and save their little princess.'

'What the hell is wrong with you?' I said contemptuously. Attack was the best form of defense.

'You're a thief, Layla.'

My cheeks flamed, but I was not giving up so easily. 'I'm not,' I cried hotly.

'You have nothing to fear then. Call your brother,' he invited.

I bit my lip. 'Look. I'm sorry I was in your bedroom. I'll just go downstairs and we won't spoil anybody else's night, OK?'

'OK.'

My mouth dropped open at my effortless victory. I closed it shut. 'Thank you,' I said quickly.

'After you admit that you stole and... I've punished you.'

A bark of incredulity tore out of my mouth. 'What?'

'The problem with you, Layla, is that you were never spanked when you were young. Your Da and Jake were much too much in love with you to execute any kind of discipline over you. As a consequence you have grown up an unruly weed.'

My eyes narrowed suspiciously. I knew it. I always knew it. He was low enough to blackmail me? This was the proof I had been looking for—that he was just low, low, low. He had always been low and he would always be low. 'What kind of punishment are you talking about, you?'

'You should have what you have never had... A spanking.' His tone was terrifyingly pleasant.

I stared at him in disbelief.

He raised an eyebrow.

'How dare you—?' I began.

But he interrupted me coldly. 'This is getting boring. The choice is simple. You apologize and submit to a spanking, or we call your brother—or, if you prefer, your mother.'

Jake? My mother? The pseudo fury drained out of me like water from a sink plug. I worried my bottom lip and thought of my mother's eyes dimming with humiliation and my brother staring at me without comprehension. He had given me the best of everything. When we were young and poor my mother said Jake would always forgo his share of something if I wanted it.

My actions were inexcusable. I had thoroughly disgraced and dishonored our family. I had walked into a Pilkington's bedroom and stolen something from it like a common thief. Now that I thought about it, even I had no idea why I had done it. I had never done anything like that before. It was the stupidest, maddest thing I had ever done.

My gaze slid to his large hand, jerked back to his tanned face. 'You wouldn't!'

'Why wouldn't I?' he clipped.

Physical punishment for me, or mental anguish for both Ma and Jake. I swallowed hard. 'No,' I whispered. 'I'll take the...punishment.'

'Great,' he said softly and, taking a step forward, kicked the door shut with his heel. He was so big. So meaty. Suddenly the room seemed so much smaller. He was like a predatory animal. Instinctively, I took a corresponding step backwards. My eyes strayed to his hands. God, they were baseball mitts.

'How do we do this?' My voice was clear and matter-of-fact. I had to assert some sort of control.

'I'll sit on the bed. You will position yourself on my lap. I will raise your skirt and spank you. Eight times.'

Raise my skirt! I felt heat creep over my body. Oh, the shame of it. But if I was honest there was something else, something dark and hot. Something I'd never dreamed would happen to me. How could I be turned on by his depraved idea of a punishment? I looked into his eyes. They were blank mirrors. There was nothing to see, only what I was. A thief.

But as I stared into his eyes, I saw a flash of something old. And suddenly I knew. This humiliation was not punishment because I had come into his bedroom and stolen his tiepin. It was because of what had happened when I was thirteen years old. I had tripped over a tree root and fallen down. My skirt had come up and my panties had showed. I could remember them even now. They were white cotton with red polka dots. And all the other kids and BJ had seen them. I had wanted to jump up but I was too winded to move.

Some of the kids had laughed. I knew they were afraid of Jake and they would never have laughed if BJ had not been there. At that time our families—BJ's and mine—were in a generational feud. It was only recently that Jake and BJ had uprooted the barbed fences between our families. Since everybody knew about our feud they had thought they could ingratiate themselves with him by laughing at me.

But in a flash he had come up to me and helped me up. Even then he was a big lad with a Mohican hairstyle, and the other kids were scared of him. They had immediately ceased laughing then.

'Are you all right?' he had asked.

I had been so mortally embarrassed that it was him who should have witnessed my humiliation that I had lashed out at him. 'Take your dirty hands off me, you filthy Pilkington, you,' I snapped.

He had gone bright red and jerked his hand away from me.

I had turned on my heel and limped away on my twisted ankle. I knew he was watching me but I didn't give him the satisfaction of turning back to look. After that we became enemies. And now he had caught me in his bedroom.

Finally, he could exact his revenge. He walked past me, sat on his bed and turning to me said, 'Ready when you are.'

You might also like to check out
Crystal Jake - The Best Selling EDEN
series Box Set.
http://www.amazon.com/Crystal-Jake-
Complete-EDEN-Series-
ebook/dp/B00X2JUCRC

http://www.amazon.co.uk/Crystal-
Jake-Complete-EDEN-Series-
ebook/dp/B00X2JUCRC

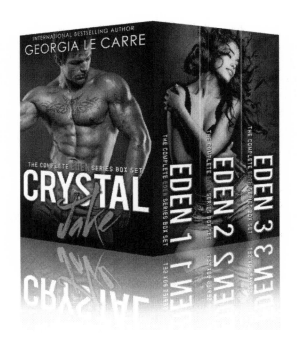

Coming Soon...

GOLD DIGGER

Georgia Le Carre

CHAPTER 1

'**W**hatever you do, don't *ever* trust them. Not one of them,' he whispered. His voice was so feeble I had to strain to catch it.

'I won't,' I said, softly.

'They are dangerous in a way you will never understand. Never let your guard down,' he insisted.

'I understand,' I said, but all I wanted was for him to stop talking about them. These last precious minutes I didn't want to waste on them.

He shook his head unhappily. 'No, no, you don't understand. You can never let your guard down for even an instant. Never.'

'All right, I won't.'

'I will be a very sad spirit if you do.'

'I won't,' I promised vehemently, and reached for his hand. The contrast between my hand and his couldn't have been greater. Mine was smooth and soft and his was gnarled and full of green veins, the skin waxy and liver-spotted. The nails were the color of polished ivory. The hand of a seventy-year-old man. His fingers grasped fiercely at my hand. I lifted them to my lips and kissed them one by one, tenderly.

His eyes glowed briefly in his wasted, sunken face. 'How I love you, my darling Tawny,' he murmured.

'I love you. I love you. I love you,' I said.

'Do your part and they cannot touch you.'

He sighed. 'It's nearly time.'

'Don't say that,' I cried, even though I knew in my heart that he was right.

His eyes swung to the window. 'Ah,' he sighed softly. 'You've come.'

My gaze chased his. The window he was looking at was closed, the heavy drapes pulled shut. Goose pimples crawled up my arms. 'Don't go yet. Please,' I begged.

He dragged his gaze reluctantly from the window. His thin, pale lips rose at the edges as he drew in a rattling breath. 'I've got to go, my darling. I've got to pay my dues. I haven't been a good man.'

'Just wait a while.'

'You have your whole life ahead of you.'

He turned his unnaturally bright eyes away from me, looked straight ahead, and with a violent shudder, departed.

For a few seconds I simply stared at him. Appropriately, outside the October wind howled and dashed itself into the shutters. I knew the servants were waiting downstairs.

Everyone was waiting for me to go down and tell them the news. Then I leaned forward and put my cheek on his still, bony chest. He smelled strongly of medicine. I closed my eyes tightly. Why did you have to go and die and leave me to the wolves?

In that moment I felt so close to him I wished that this time would not end. I wished I could lie on his chest, safe and closeted away from the cruel world. I heard the clock ticking. The flames in the fireplace crackled and spat. Somewhere a pipe creaked. I placed my chin on his chest and turned to look at him one last time. He appeared to be sleeping. Peaceful at any rate. I stroked the thin strands of white hair lying across his pinkish white scalp, and let my finger run down his prominent nose. It shocked me how quickly the tip of his nose had lost warmth. Soon all of him would be stone cold.

I wondered whom he had seen at the window. Who had come to take him to his reckoning. My sorrow was complete. I could put my fingertips into it and feel the edges. Smooth. Without corners. Without sharpness. It had no tears. I knew he was dying two hours before. Strange because it had seemed as if he had taken a turn for the better. He seemed stronger, his cheeks pink, his eyes brilliantly bright and when he smiled it appeared as if he was lit from within. He even looked so much stronger. I asked him what he wanted to eat.

'Milk. I'll have a glass of milk,' he said decisively.

But after I called for milk and it was brought to him he smiled and refused it. 'Isn't this wonderful?' he asked. 'I feel so good.'

And at that moment I knew. Even so it was incomprehensible to me that he was really gone. I never wanted to believe it.

'In the end you wanted to go, didn't you?'

There was no answer.

'It's OK. I know you were tired. It was only me holding you back. You go on ahead. Find a place for me.'

He lay as still as a corpse. Oh God! I already missed him so much.

'I understand you can't talk. But you can hear me. When it is my turn I want you to come and get me. I'll be expecting you to come in through the window. Go in peace now, my love. All will be well. They will never know the truth. I will never tell them. To the day you come back to collect me.'

And then I began to cry, not loud, ugly sobs, but a quiet weeping. I didn't want the servants to hear. To come rushing in. Call the doctor waiting downstairs to come in and pronounce him dead. I knew what waited for me outside this room. Another hour...or two wouldn't make a difference. This was my time. My final hours with my husband.

The time before I became the hated gold digger.